|2/2| **DATE DUE**

p us Rate this book...
t your initials on the
side and your rating
on the right side.

l = Didn't care for
  2 = It was O.K.
  3 = It was <u>great</u>

_____ 1 2 3
_____ 1 2 3
_____ 1 2 3
_____ 1 2 3
_____ 1 2 3
_____ 1 2 3
_____ 1 2 3
_____ 1 2 3
_____ 1 2 3
_____ 1 2 3
_____ 1 2 3
_____ 1 2 3
_____ 1 2 3
_____ 1 2 3

DISCARDED

PRINTED IN U.S.A.

The Sheriff

Center Point
Large Print

**This Large Print Book carries the
Seal of Approval of N.A.V.H.**

WEST OF THE BIG RIVER

The Sheriff

*A Novel Based on the Life of
Commodore Perry Owens*

CHUCK TYRELL

CENTER POINT LARGE PRINT
THORNDIKE, MAINE

The Sheriff

Foreword

Commodore Perry Owens

I'd seen the Albuquerque tintype and I'd read the newspaper account of the Blevins-Cooper shootout, but I still wasn't ready for the cold hard stare and careful stance that met me when I pushed through the batwings of the Bucket of Blood.

I took off my hat and approached the bar. The man with the stare and the stance moved three steps down the bar, keeping a ten-foot space between him and myself. "I'm Alexander Evanston," I said, "from the Phoenix Sun."

"You the reporter?" said the man at the corner of the bar. He wore a gray handlebar moustache and a white apron wrapped around his more-than-ample girth.

"I am," I said. "I sent a letter some weeks ago, asking for an opportunity to interview Commodore Perry Owens."

The man with the hard stare spoke. "Got anything that says you're what you say you are?" he asked.

"I do. Mr. Robinson, our publisher, supplies us with business cards for just such occasions."

7

I fished one from my vest pocket and placed it on the bar. The man with the hard eyes extended his hand. The barman pulled the card to the edge of the bar with his index finger, caught it with his thumb as it hit the edge, and with it pinched between finger and thumb, handed it to the hard man.

"Phoenix Sun, eh? All the news that is news, without fear or favor, eh?"

"Yes, sir," I said.

"How come you to work for the Phoenix Sun?"

"I graduated from Stanford with a degree in education," I said, "but what I really like to do is write. Mr. Robinson is an old friend of my father's, and he offered me a job on the paper. Now I am here, sir."

"School larned, eh?"

"Yes, sir. But now I'm learning the real world, and letting our readers know exactly what I find out."

The hard man may have smiled, but it looked like a smirk. "Three years, all told," he said.

"Three years, sir?"

"Yeah. Three years of schooling. That's all I ever got."

"Times are changing, sir. A man best get an education, if he can."

The hard man glanced down at the toes of his boots, then watched a wagon rattle by the saloon toward Main Street. He flinched at a backfire and cast a baleful eye on the passing Model T Ford. "Damn horseless carriages," he said. "Near as bad as telephones. And you're right, shaver. Times are changing, for a fact. Today ain't nothing like what used to be."

A man burst through the batwings and clomped to the bar. "Usual," he said.

The barman drew him a beer and slid it across the bar. Some of the foam sloshed out and left a streak on the shiny bar.

"Hey. Careful. Don' waste m'beer."

The barman grinned. "You know I fill it extra full for you, Dave. Don't bitch so much."

"So what if I bitch. C.P. gonna fill me up with lead if I do?"

"He might just do that. Never can tell."

Dave lifted his beer mug to the hard-eyed man. "C.P.," he said, "you reckon I've got the right to bitch in the golmighty Bucket of Blood?"

My eyes whipped from Dave to the hard man. So this was the famous Commodore Perry Owens. Said to have killed fourteen men and wounded half a hundred more. He nodded in my direction and motioned toward a table in the back. "We'll talk over there," he said, shutting beer-drinker Dave out of the conversation.

"Fine," I said, and moved over to the table Owens had indicated. He strode to the far end of the bar, and arrived at the table with a sawed-off shotgun in his right hand. He sat opposite me and put the shotgun on the seat of the chair next to him.

"Why the scattergun?" I asked.

"How many people over sixty do you know, son?"

I thought. "Not all that many."

"Well, I'm a year past sixty, and part of the reason is that I'm careful. Always careful."

The barman brought a sudsy glass of something for Owens. "What'll you have?" he said to me.

"Beer?"

The barman gave me a curt nod, and went back to the bar.

"Now what is it you want to talk to me about, Evanston?"

"Well, sir . . ."

"I ain't no sir, son. Just C.P., or Commodore, as you please."

"Commodore, then?"

"That'd be fine. Now, what was it you wanted to talk about?"

"Well. These days it seems that Wyatt Earp, that Tombstone lawman, is getting all the attention. I looked at Arizona lawmen when I was at Stanford," I said. "I read about Bob Paul and Burton Mossman, some about Texas John Slaughter, too. But you, sir, I mean Commodore, seemed to me to have done more than just about any other lawman in Arizona history to turn this wild territory into one ready to be a state."

10

"We're a state, son, without no help from me." Owens took a sip from his glass, and I from mine.

"Could I hear about you, Commodore, from your very own lips?"

"Dunno that I have any kind of a story to tell, son, not much of one, anyway."

"I heard you were born in Tennessee. Is that right?"

"That's right. But we moved to Indiana right after. My folks were Quakers. They didn't take to slaveholding. I always thought they moved north to get out of slave country, the war coming on and all."

"How long did you live in Indiana?"

Owens rubbed his hand across his mouth, smoothing his moustache down with his index finger. "Some of my folks still live there," he said.

"But you came west."

"Things wasn't good after the war. Back then, a boy of twelve or thirteen was a man growed. I left home when I was thirteen."

I scribbled shorthand in my notebook.

Owens watched. "Funny writing," he said. "But then, I don't write so good, so what can I say?"

"It's called shorthand, Commodore. Faster than regular writing. I don't want to miss anything you say." I steered the conversation back to where we left off. "You left home at thirteen, then."

"Yes."

Silence. Somewhere outside the damned Model

11

T was backfiring again. Owens must have been used to the sound because he didn't flinch or move his hand toward the shotgun. He just sat there like he'd answered my question in full.

"Right," I said. "Where did you go? Wasn't the war in full swing about then?"

"No. Just over."

I watched him. He looked at the edge of the table. Then he inspected the chandeliers hanging in the Bucket of Blood. He leaned over to check the shotgun. He laced his fingers together and put the backs of his hands against his chest. He frowned. I wondered if the interview was over.

"Just over," he said again, "and riverboats needed boys to fire their boilers. A man can stay out of sight for a long time in riverboats. Nobody knows any different. No one knows if I was there or not. I was, but nobody knows, and neither do you."

I wrote a line.

"I didn't like boats," he said. "I left when it was safe. Went to the Nations. Learned how to cowboy. Learned about horses. Learned how to shoot."

"May I ask where in the Nations?"

"Here'n there. Did some trailing on the Goodnight. Hunted some buffalo for the Atchison Topeka. Cowboyed on the Rogers' spread. Cherokees're good cowmen. Good riflemen, too. Yeah. Learned a lot in the Nations. Hil Rogers

12

died in '71, but Will—that's his boy—Will kept me on."

"Sounds exciting," I said, hoping that Owens would tell me some exciting experiences.

"Things people call exciting happen when a man drinks or gambles, usually. I don't drink, and I don't gamble. A man gets ahead if he works hard, that's what I say."

"Cowboying's hard work, I'd say. Does it get a man ahead?"

"We didn't think so in the Nations. We truly did not. Lots of people was making extra money hauling spirits into the Nations, mostly from Texas. We figured we was tough customers. Yeah, there was a law against taking booze into the Nations, but it happened every day. The Cherokees knew it. The Choctaw knew it. The Kiowa knew it. Well, we got caught. Twice. That put me up before Judge Isaac Parker. I wasn't gonna lie. He said I was accused of hauling spirits into the Nations, how did I plead. I said, 'Guilty.'

"Judge Parker's known as a hanging judge. He don't go lenient. And he weren't lenient on me. I got caught twice, and he sentenced me to three months in jail for each offense, and he fined me a hundred dollars twice. Cowboying don't make a man rich, but neither does shipping whiskey into the Indian Nations." Owens looked like he'd eaten something bitter and sour.

I didn't say anything after I'd written down what he'd said. Owens wasn't a talker and certainly wasn't a braggart. At least as far as I could see.

"Pays not to break the law," Owens said.

"But you've never been an outlaw, have you?"

Owens snorted. "Bunch of us young'uns figured we was hot back in the '70s. We done a lot of talking, mostly amongst ourselves. We talked about hawking whiskey. Talked about making off with some good horses. Even talked about holding up trains. Talk. Talk. Talk. Maybe if I'd not been sent up by Judge Parker. Maybe if we'd done what we talked about. Then maybe I'd have rode the Outlaw Trail. Who knows?"

"But you didn't."

Owens cracked a slight grin. "No, I didn't. Soon as I got out, I left. Never talked to the old gang again. Weren't worth it."

"Where'd you go then?"

"West."

"West from Oklahoma?"

"Straight west. Clipped Colorado on the corner and dropped straight into New Mexico. Spent a little time in Santa Fe, but the beaver days and the trade with Mexico was gone, so I drifted south to Albuquerque. That's where I met Houck."

"Do you mean James Houck, the man who was your deputy?"

"That's him. Hadn't I of met Jim Houck, I'd

14

never of come to Arizona in the first place. But he kept going on about belly-high grass on the Colorado Plateau and how the Apaches never raided and the Navajos could be taken care of. He painted such a good picture, and me wanting to homestead a place to raise horses, him and I decided to ride west towards Apache County in Arizona."

"I heard that Commodore Perry Owens horses were something to be sought. Is that right?"

"I tried. Kept some good stock. Rode the best I had. Rode one to death, in fact. Not supposed to do that to blooded horses, you know. Grass up around Navajo and Commodore Springs was right good for my horses."

A group of men pushed into the Bucket of Blood. They lined the bar and started trading stabs with the barman. Commodore kept his attention on the men until they had their drinks and had settled down a bit. "Where were we?" he asked as he turned back to me.

"I think we were talking about James Houck and blooded horses, Commodore," I said. "What kind of horses did you raise?"

"Well, I was lucky enough to get me a half-Thoroughbred, half-Arabian mare that was from Keene Richard's stock. I rode her into Arizona from Albuquerque, me and Jim together. He said Apache County was booming and that it was the place a man could make something of himself.

Convinced me. I was happy to ride along. Happy to get a cowboying and remuda guard job with Jim's pa. A man's nothing without work, ya know."

"When did you arrive in Arizona, if I may ask?"

"Let me think. I reckon it was the spring of '81. Yeah. Wells Fargo ran a stage up from Tucson and over to Diablo and they held a herd of nags at Navajo Springs. They called it Navajo Springs, but it's just a seep. Dug a ditch into the bog so water could seep in and clear up for the horses. Worked good, and there was always plenty of graze."

"Navajo Springs is not all that far from Carrizo Creek, is it?"

"I know what you're getting at, boy. Navajos. Well, they figured all the country south of Lithodendron Wash and the Painted Desert all the way to the Zuni River was theirs, and maybe it was at one time. But you know Colonel Carson took the Navajo Indians to Redondo in '64. They wasn't never the same after that. J. L. Hubbell had him a trading post up north of Window Rock. Still, them Navajos liked to get away with a horse whenever they could. We just had to go on after 'em and take 'em back."

Part I

Of Horses and Navajos

C. P. Owens was a careful man, but a man willing to talk as well. It seemed somehow that he wanted to set the record straight rather that have it overblown, or underblown, as the case may be. He spoke well, though without a lawyer's learning, and I have decided to use my volumes of notes from those few days in Seligman, Arizona, to allow C.P. (I ended up calling him C.P., like everyone else) to tell his own story.

1

The days before I got to Arizona don't mean a lot. What I'm saying is, well, I learned cowboying at the Rogers Ranch in Oklahoma, and I came near to becoming an outlaw while I was in the Nations, too. Those days are not important to the real Commodore Perry Owens. I reckon my life began the day I crossed the line from New Mexico into Arizona. Me and Jim Houck rode all the way from Albuquerque where I first made his acquaintance. Jim had a temper and sometimes he had a short trigger, but he was straight as an arrow, and when he gave his word, it was good to the grave. Anyhow, Jim was always raving on about how good the country in Arizona was, with grama grass up to a horse's belly and land easy to get from the Atlantic & Pacific Railroad. I had no ties where I come from, Judge Parker'd caught me to rights on the whiskey to the Indians thing, and I was shy of breaking any kind of law anywhere—another reason it was easy for Jim Houck to talk me into riding to Arizona.

The good thing about riding into Arizona from the east is the weather. I was on my dappled gray, leading a bay Morgan. Jim had a short-coupled lineback dun and black-pointed buckskin. We rode through the gap between Mount Powell and

Castle Rock to the north and the Zuni Mountains to the south. We spent a night at Gallup, a new town astraddle the A&P Railroad. Jim got rousing drunk at the Pine Picket Saloon and I had to just about carry him back to the horses. Me, I don't drink none. Never have, even though I was jailed for selling liquor to Indians in the Nations.

Hung over as Jim was, dawn still saw us out of our soogans and huddled over a hatful of fire, frying sowbelly and making a bit of frybread. The sun was just coming up when we stomped the fire out, rolled up our soogans and tarps, saddled up, tied our rolls behind the cantles, and pointed the noses of our mounts toward Navajo Springs, riding west on the Beale Wagon Road. We didn't worry about Indians at the time, and made it to Navajo Springs stage station with no trouble.

Fred Adams came out of the stage station just as me and Jim rode up. "Howdy," he said. "See any Navajos on your way in?"

"Nope," Jim said. "All right to use the water?"

"Damned Navajos run off with three head of Fargo horses," Fred said. "Hep yourself."

He walked along as we went to the pond for water. Navajo Springs is rightly a seep. Water comes up in a little swale and makes a pond about fifty feet across. Funny thing is, that water never gets stagnant so there's probably some kind of underground stream beneath the pond.

"No Navajos, eh?" Fred was almighty set on us having noticed Indian sign or something.

"Nary a one," I said, "but we wasn't particular looking out for Indians. Easy riding along that Beale Wagon Road. Near snoozed all the way over from Gallup."

Fred snorted. "I'll bet," he said. "I've known Jim Houck since he was knee-high to a grasshopper, but I don't recollect you." He squatted at the edge of the pond and pulled a grass stem to chew on.

"He's a top hand," Jim said, nodding his head at me. "Worked some years on that big Rogers Ranch in Oklahoma. Name's Commodore. Commodore Perry Owens."

"Hell of a name," Fred said.

"It's the one my ma and pa saddled me with," I said. "I reckon it will have to do. You can call me C.P. if that makes things easier."

"C.P., eh? That'll do. C.P. you are."

"Obliged for the water," Jim said. "We'll ride on over to the ranch. I been away a while and the old man don't know I'm coming. Surprise, I'd say." He chuckled. "Come on, Commodore, let's ride."

"Good to know you, Fred," I said. "I'll be around, I reckon. Maybe we'll meet up somewhere."

"So long," said Fred. He turned back toward the station house. Then he hollered at us as we rode on west toward Jim's dad's ranch. "Hey, you all. If you need a job, you can hire on here and go get them horses back from the Induns."

We hied on down the road toward the Houck ranch, Jim talking up a storm and me thinking about the flat condition of my wallet, if I'd of had a wallet.

"Jim? Jim? Is that you, Jim?" The girl who came running out of the ranch house was comely and dressed modestly. Jim piled off his horse and she flang both arms around his neck and give him a kiss that probably made the hair on the back of his neck stand up. When they got through smooching, Jim turned to me. The girl hung on to his arm.

"Commodore, this here's my wife, Bessie," he said. "We ain't been married even a year yet."

" 'Bout time you come home, Jim." The statement come from a tall man, a little stooped in the shoulders with some white showing in his sideburns.

"Pa! Pa! How in hell you been doing?"

The man came up short. "James. I know you've been gone for some weeks, but we don't go for swearing at this ranch. You know that."

Jim ducked his head like a kid. "Sorry, Pa," he said. Bessie stood off to the side, but I could tell by the look on her face that Jim Houck was gonna be awful busy keeping her satisfied, at least for a while.

"Pa," he said, "this here's Commodore Perry Owens. He cowboyed for the Rogers' outfit in the Nations, and him and me met up in Albuquerque. He was looking for a place he might like, and I told him Arizona was as near to heaven as he was likely to get here on earth. He come along to see for himself."

"Howdy, Commodore," Jim's pa said. "If Jim says you're a cowboy, most likely you are. What do you figure on doing here?"

That's when I made my mind up. "Seems Fred Adams needs someone to go look for some Fargo horses," I said. "I'll just shamble on over to Navajo Springs and see if I can't get them horses back for him. Looks like Jim's got some catching up to do here at home. I'll come back by to see what's going on after I've found them plugs."

"No need to rush off," Jim said, but his eyes was on Bessie.

"You know me, Jim. Gotta be doing something. Fred sounded like he wanted some help and I'm footloose. I'll just go back and talk to him, maybe sign on for a while."

"Git off that hoss," Jim said. "You need something to eat."

It was too early for supper. "Cup of coffee would be good," I said. "Then I'll git along over to Navajo Springs." I dismounted and tied my two horses to the front hitching rail. Jim was already in the house, and I figured maybe he didn't want me busting in on him.

"Jim say you worked for the Rogers' spread?" Jim's pa was still outside, too.

"I did. Spent half a dozen years or so there."

"Uh huh." He wanted to hear more, but I wasn't talking. That judge in the Nations had me not wanting to talk too much about bygones.

"Don't mind working with dogies, but I'm right fond of horses," I said. "That's one reason why I'm gonna go back to see Fred Adams at Navajo Springs. Don't think he wants to lose them Fargo horses."

"This here's good horse country, and there's a prime place over to Cottonwood Seep. Be a good homestead because it's off railroad land."

"That right? Maybe I'll have a look at it after I get the horses back."

"Be glad to show you around. Come on back when you get a chance." Jim's pa was right friendly, but then, in those days people didn't come around to visit very often. Then Jim and Bessie came out with a coffee pot and cups for me and Jim's pa, and good coffee it was.

It was less than ten miles from the Houck outfit to Navajo Springs, so I got back some time before sundown. Nobody out front, so I hollered. "Hello, the house. Anybody home?"

Fred Adams come outta the station house

24

wiping his hands on a flour sack. "Hey, you'll be C.P.," he said.

"I will be. You still want me to go get those Fargo horses back for you?"

"You can do that?"

"I can give her a good try. I learned a bit about trailing and tracking in the Nations, working with Chickasaw and Cherokee." I climbed off my gray. "Could I hobble this gray and turn him loose around here? Or would the Navajo make off with him?"

"Should be all right."

I put the rig on my hefty Morgan and stripped the Winchester out of the saddle scabbard. "Borrow a seat for a while? I'll clean my Remington and my Winchester before I light out after them Navajos," I said.

Fred had a good look at my Winchester when I set it on a table while I dug the cleaning stuff outta my saddlebag. "That there's a one-in-a-thousand '76, ain't it?"

"Reckon so."

"Cost seventy-five dollars over to Saint Johns. I seen one there. They say them rifles shoot awful straight."

I gave Fred a nod. "That gun puts the bullet wherever I point it. But if I don't point it at the right thing, it don't hit nothing. What I'm saying is, it ain't the rifle what shoots straight, it's the man pulling the trigger."

"No shit."

"I can hit what I point that rifle at. That's for sure. Now. Where'd be a good place to start looking for them lost Fargo horses?"

"Best chance would be going north till you hit Bonito Creek. Look around there for prints with lugs on the shoes. All the Fargo horses got lugs on their shoes, front and back."

I gave him a short nod and went to cleaning my weapons. Fred just sat there and watched. A man's guns, long and short, gotta work every time he pulls the trigger else life'll get mighty short. Going after those horses, I might need firepower bad. I was making sure I had it when I needed it.

Finished, I put the weapons back in their holsters and went out to hobble my dapple so he could graze but not get too far away. "Got any grain, Fred?" I hollered.

"Some."

"Oughta give my Morgan some before going to look for the Fargo horses. Spare a bait?"

Fred didn't look happy, but he went into the stable and got a *morral* of oats for Morg. While the bay was eating, I took a look around. Sure enough, all the stage horses had lugs on their shoes. Didn't help a man tell one stage nag from another, but the tracks would stick out like a sore thumb on some creek bank.

Back at the station, I asked Fred where the

horses had been when the Indians took them.

"Funny thing," he said. "They was right there in the holding corral. Had two span put in there for a change when the stage come in. Them Induns took three of 'um."

"Why not all four?"

"When you ketch up with 'um, you can ast 'um."

Lot of help Fred Adams was. I threw a leg over Morg's back and we started making circles around Navajo Springs. If you get up on a little rise anywhere around Navajo Springs, you can see quite a ways. Off to the south there were a few hills, and the Little Colorado River wasn't too far off to the north. I was on my third circle around the stage station, widening out the part to the north every time I went around, when I come across the trail of six horses. Three ponies and three big horses with lugs on their shoes. The ponies wore shoes, but I knew from the Nations that Indians put shoes on their horses whenever they could, usually at some reservation Indian agent place. Me and Morg, we just naturally followed those tracks.

The six horses moved north and a little east from Navajo Springs stage station. I had no trouble tracking them to the Puerco River, and though they waded upstream in the shallows for some distance, I found where they left the river, crossed the A&P Railroad tracks, and headed up a wash that dribbled a little water. Later I found out they called it Carrizo Creek.

Horse droppings and so on along the trail told me the Navajos were about two hours ahead of me, and as I didn't know the country, all I could do was stick to that trail. Off to the west, hills and mesas and washes rolled away in a riot of colors that's a little hard for an uneducated cowboy to explain. I heard an army man by the name of Ives called it the Painted Desert. I believe it. It was all red and white and purple and pink, and when the sun hit it just right, it surely looked like all of the good Lord's angels had taken to them hills with paint brushes. But I was chasing Navajos who'd stole Wells Fargo horses, so I didn't spend much time thinking about beautiful scenery.

That Navajo land is a hard one. Never any extra water. Not much moisture falls from the skies. There was a trickle of water in Carrizo Creek, so me and Morg had no problem with drying out. Still, we didn't catch up with the Fargo horses until the morning of the third day.

2

Kit Carson and the army took a big bunch of Navajos off to Bosque Redondo in east New Mexico back in '64. But they were back now. I didn't know much about Navajos, but my years in the Nations let me see how red men think. And most of them think in terms of horses when calculating the worth of a man. The three Fargo horses those Navajos was leading into Navajo territory meant a good deal. Not only the worth of a horse, but the worth of a horse stole from the white eyes.

I followed the tracks of the stolen horses until it got too dark to see them anymore. I found a good patch of grass, staked Morg where he could eat all he wanted of that good grass, and set down to a dry camp. Were I off Indian land, I'd have built a fire for coffee and maybe a bit of frybread, but out here with only myself for company, I made no fires.

The night was cold in that high dry country, but I always carry a blanket and my slicker, so it wasn't all that bad. I had a bit of bacon and some hardtack, so I dined somewhat like a king, meaning that I didn't starve. I even managed to catch a wink or two while Morg stood guard.

Dawn came early, so I was on the trail of

those Fargo horses nearly an hour before the sun showed its face. I reckon those Navajo braves figured they was nigh home, because they made not a single attempt to hide those lug-shoe hoofprints, or go by any roundabout way. And that beeline of hoofprints went straight to Emigrant Springs.

Not far from there's where I seen the first Navajo.

The land around Emigrant Springs ain't all that rough. And where there's permanent water, there's bound to be some kind of camp or settlement nearby. Now your plains Indian, Cheyenne or even Comanche, he'll live in a teepee. But the Navajo, he settles permanent-like, and builds him a hogan, usually six-sided walls of juniper logs fitted one on top of the other and packed with adobe mud all around. Well, I'd never seen a Navajo hogan before, even though I spent some months in New Mexico.

Up on the flat north of Emigrant Springs, there was four of those squat hogans. Couldn't see no one around, but that didn't mean no one was there. A man only sees a Indian if the Indian wants him to. Leastwise that's how I always found it. Besides, one of those mudhut-looking hogans had smoke coming out the top. That meant someone was home. But there were no horses. And no dogs. Made a man wonder if anyone actually lived in them hogans.

I let Morg drink his fill at the pool below the springs. I sipped from my canteen while he was drinking, then pulled my Winchester '76 from its scabbard, just in case.

No one came out of the hogans, but them being Indians, I figured they—if there was anyone home—they'd know I was there.

Sure enough, the minute I turned Morg's head toward the hogans, a man come out from behind the wool blanket that served for a door. He held a single-shot Springfield in the crook of his left arm. I held my Winchester across the saddle bows.

He let me ride up close, but there could have been someone else watching from somewhere. It's hard to spot an Indian what don't want to be spotted.

Up close, I saw that the man was old enough to have streaks of gray in his black hair, which he wore long and tied in a kind of bun at the back of his head.

"Looking for stole horses," I said, raising my voice so the old man could hear.

He shook his head.

I didn't know if he meant that he couldn't hear me or that he didn't understand. Maybe both. I snicked at Morg, and he took a couple of steps toward the Navajo, head up and ears pricked forward. Morg's attention was focused on the old man, so I figured there might not be anyone else close around. Certainly not the horse thieves.

"Horses!" I hollered.

The old man just shook his head.

I touched a finger to the brim of my hat to salute the old man, then went back to Emigrant Springs to look for the tracks of those lug-shoed Fargo horses.

The tracks were there, but they didn't lead to the hogans. Instead, they sidled off to the east and took a little arroyo that could well have hidden them from view of the hogans. At least if no one was looking, no one would have noticed.

I was after the Fargo horses, so I followed the tracks. Simple as that. And them what took the horses weren't expecting nobody to come after them, so they took no pains to hide the tracks.

A little over two miles on, I topped a little rise and looked down on a pretty little swale. I say little, but it was well over a hundred acres in size. There must have been underground water there because the grass of the swale was belly high to a 16-hand horse. I could tell because there was twenty-three head of stock grazing in that swale. Three of them were the Fargo horses. They still had their halters on and they were the only horses in sight with harness marks on their hides.

Two Navajo boys rode herd on the horses. They carried boy-sized bows and a few arrows.

I reined Morg around the edge of the swale

32

rather than ride him through the horse herd. I knew a bit of the Indian sign language what they called hand talk, and I hoped it would let me talk to those boys. I truly did not want to have to shoot either one of them.

The boys came together on the far side of the herd as Morg and I started around. I signed that I came in peace.

They ignored my hands. Maybe Navajos didn't know the hand patois of the plains.

I kept Morg moving around the edge of the herd, which ignored me. Good grass was a lot more important to them than a lone rider who made no dangerous-looking moves.

One of the boys nocked an arrow and moved his pony so he was facing the direction I came from. The other boy retreated back around the swale, putting fifty or sixty yards between himself and the other boy.

I signed "peace" again.

The boy with the nocked arrow watched me through squinted eyes.

At the place nearest the Fargo horses, I dismounted.

The Navajo boy's pony did a nervous dance. I signed "peace" again, then took my lariat from the saddle.

The pony danced closer.

I ignored the boy and walked to the Fargo horses, talking nonsense to them in a soothing voice. In no time, I had all three linked together with the lariat. They'd follow, trusting the years of training they'd gotten pulling Wells Fargo stagecoaches across Arizona.

The boy with the nocked arrow screeched as I started to move the Fargo horses away from the herd. I signed "peace" and "my horses."

He gigged the pony around the herd in my direction. I ignored him and mounted Morg. I took the retaining loop off the hammer of my Remington. I didn't want to kill that boy, but he could kill me just as easy and just as dead as could a full-grown warrior. What's more, the herd was his responsibility and I had cut out three of what to his mind were his horses. To him, I was the horse thief, not the other way around.

"*Tai akwai-i,*" he shouted, bow drawn and nocked arrow at his cheek. "*Tai akwai-i!*"

He let the arrow fly and I naturally palmed my Remington, cocking it as it cleared the holster, and shot him in the chest. Wasn't time to do anything else.

The boy toppled from his pony. I didn't stop to see if he was dead. I hauled on the lariat lead line to those Fargo horses and made for Navajo Springs as quick as I knew how.

The other boy didn't chase me. Maybe he was too young. Probably not more than six or seven years old.

Me and the Fargo horses, we headed back the

way we come, taking almost the same trail back as we did coming to Emigrant Springs. The Fargo horses were used to running and so was Morg, so we made it almost to the A&P Railroad tracks before the first bullets from irate Navajos crashed in.

Don't know if they was too mad to hit what they shot at or what, but none of that Navajo lead seemed to even come close. Morg and me hit a gallop, and the Fargo horses came right along behind. 'Course they wasn't pulling a ton of stagecoach either.

Once we got across the tracks, I pulled the '76 from its scabbard and snapped a shot or two at the Navajos, without really taking aim. They hollered, and pulled back on their own reins, giving me and Morg and the Fargo horses a little more time.

On the south side of the tracks, an arroyo ran down towards the Puerco River, and it was deep enough to hide me and the horses from the five or six Navajos chasing after us. As soon as Morg took me out of sight below the rim of that arroyo, I piled off, leaving the lead rope to the Fargo horses tied to Morg's saddle horn. I snaked up to the edge of the arroyo and waited for a Navajo to come into sight.

They were a bit hesitant to follow me because I'd dropped out of sight. I'd took my hat off and weighted it down with a hunk of sandstone so its shape and color would not stick out and show the warriors where I was. My hair's pert near sandy in color anyway, so I don't reckon my head stuck out all that much. Leastwise, it didn't seem like the Navajos knew precisely where I was.

The '76 had a shell in the chamber, and its hammer was eared back, so all I had to do was wriggle it between two rocks so it was pointing Navajo way.

A bullet spanged off a rock about six inches from my head and sprayed me with chips of sandstone. A puff of smoke showed where the shot had come from, but that meant little. Any fighting man knows he's got to change positions after a shot, or stand up to a hail of lead.

I stood up.

Three puffs of smoke showed from across the tracks and bullets smacked into the sandy soil around me. I put the '76 to my shoulder and watched the land across the tracks. I seen a scrap of white on black that looked to me like a headband. I laid the '76 right in the groove and triggered it. A cloud of pink mist raised above the scrap of white for a second, then it disappeared.

I waited, standing in plain sight with my Winchester '76 at my shoulder.

A shot spanged off a rock about knee level, but off to my right by at least six inches. They weren't shooting all that good.

I put a bullet in the space between two boulders

where the puff of smoke had risen. It was a good hundred yards off, but I don't reckon I missed.

No more shots.

I waited.

After a few minutes without anyone taking potshots at me, I walked back to Morg, shoved the '76 into its scabbard, and mounted up. The Fargo horses followed along toward Navajo Springs stage station just like they knew where they was going.

3

Smoke was coming out of the pipe in the roof of the station at Navajo Springs when me and the Fargo horses topped the little rise on the north side of the swale.

No one said "boo" about us riding up and me letting the Fargo horses into the corral they came from.

Fred Adams come out of the station cabin with a egg turner in his hand. "See ya got the Fargo horses," he said.

"Looks like it."

"Any trouble?"

"None I couldn't handle."

"Good. Got some rabbit in the frypan, Owens. Like a bite?"

"Let me do for my horse. Then I'll join you."

"Don't be too long 'er I'll gobble it all up my own self." Adams cackled.

Morg enjoyed a bait of Wells Fargo oats in a honest-to-god leather and canvas nosebag, while I took a currycomb to him. Kept thinking about that little Navajo boy. Another year or two, and he would have been doing a man's work instead of riding herd on the tribe's ponies. Won't never, now, but he had no right shooting arrows at me. It wasn't like the Fargo horses belonged to him, or something. Still, he'd been awful young to have his life snatched away so suddenly.

"Owens!" Fred Adams's voice came from the station cabin. "This here rabbit ain't gonna last forever."

"Be right in," I hollered. I left Morg with the nosebag on. I'd get the cockle burrs outta his tail after I'd had a hunk or two of that fried rabbit.

"Gonna be sundown fore long," Adams said. "You gonna wanna bed down here tonight? Welcome if you wanna."

"Neighborly of you, Adams—"

"Fred."

"—Fred, and I'll take you up on it. Me and my hosses'll head back to Houck's place in the morning."

Fred dumped a couple of pieces of fried rabbit onto the plate he'd set in front of me. "Some people say fried rabbit tastes like chicken, but I can't see it."

"Let me see." I took a big bite of hind leg. He'd gotten young and tender cottontails. Not much wild meat is as tender and juicy as a young cottontail. "Tastes like cottontail bunny rabbit to me. Best wild meat they is anywhere. Well, had some mighty tasty 'gator tail once, but that ain't red meat like rabbit."

Fred bit into his own piece of rabbit, pulled off a hunk of meat, and went to chewing it up. He

39

swallowed and said, "How'd you like to kind of guard the Fargo horses? Keeping the Navajos from stealing them, if ya can, and getting 'em back if ever them Injuns make off with a head or two."

"We ain't talked money of any kind."

Fred pulled more meat off the rabbit leg with teeth that looked like yellow chisels. He chewed on that bite of meat for a long time. "Well, I can guarantee you cowboy wages—that's a dollar a day and eats—fer watching the horses. Then I reckon I can get Wells Fargo to pay a bonus for every horse got back from them thieving Navajos."

"How much bounty?"

"Dunno. Have to talk to the bosses, but I can wire them from Holbrook tomorrow if you'll stick around here for me."

"I can stick around. I been thinking about homesteading at Cottonwood Seep anyway. Stage coming in tomorrow?"

"Nah. With the railroad running, Fargo's down to three coaches a week. Not coming through till day after tomorrow."

"I'll take your cowboy wages, Fred Adams, and I'll take your bounty, whatever it is."

And that's how I came to watch over the Wells Fargo herd. Well, if you can call a dozen horses a herd, that is.

Things was quiet for almost a week, then the

Indian Agent from Fort Defiance showed up with an army captain at his side.

I wasn't at the station, because I needed to build me a cabin at Cottonwood Seep, part of proving up on a homestead. I made it simple, putting juniper posts up as walls on three sides and digging out a back wall from the hill that the cabin stood up against. It's hard work putting up a cabin, but you want something that ain't gonna blow over in a dust storm. Besides, hard work never hurt a man atall.

Andy Armijo came from the direction of Navajo Springs station, quirting his little paint pony to get every extra spurt of speed it had. He brought it to a stiff-legged hopping halt. "Señor C.P.," he hollered. "*Los Indios! Los Indios!*"

I was out front of the half-built cabin before the boy and his lathered horse pulled up. "Easy, boy. What's going on?"

"Señor. Señor. Señor Adams, he said for you to come quickly. *Por favor*, he said. Andy Armijo, you hurry to fetch Señor C.P., he said, because *el agente Indio y soldados*, they are here. *Si. Es verdad.*"

"*Momentito*," I said, using one of the Mexican words I'd learned. I whistled, and Apple the gray came running. He was the only horse I had what would come when I whistled. That said, I was teaching Morg so pretty soon I'd have two.

"Hey, Apple," I said when he trotted up.

41

He answered with a blow and a nose searching for a treat. I came to the conclusion that Apple didn't come because he loved me, he came because he always got something good. I gave him a piece of hardtack from the sackful I'd bought in Holbrook. He was satisfied that coming when I whistled meant something good.

I clipped a lead rope to his halter and we went over to where I kept tack under a tarp. A couple of minutes and we were ready to accompany Andy Armijo back to Navajo Springs. "Vamoose," I said, the cowboy equivalent of Mexican for "Let's go."

Apple's a good horse with a fairly fast gait, but Andy's little paint danced on ahead as if the party would start before he ever got there.

At Navajo Springs, I saw four horses, one with a run-of-the-mill rig and three with blue saddle blankets and those uncomfortable McClellan saddles the army likes to use. Four men.

I took Apple's bridle off so he could graze around. He'd come when I whistled. Andy'd taken his horse to the corral back of the station. He stayed there, perched on the top rail, so I knew he wasn't invited inside. Automatically, I pulled my Remington, checked the cylinder, added a bullet, and put it back in the holster that sat at my left hip. I ratcheted a shell into the chamber of my one-in-a-thousand Winchester '76. Apple went to cropping grass. I went to knock on the station cabin door, thinking it a little strange that Fred Adams wasn't out and about. Holding the '76 Apache style, lying along my left forearm, barrel up and action where my right hand would naturally take hold if the need came, I rapped on the door and Fred Adams jerked it open like he'd been standing there waiting.

"Andy said you needed me."

Fred looked uncomfortable. "Come on in," he said, and stepped back.

I went in.

The Navajo Springs station's not all that big. The major stop's in Holbrook. Here folks stretch their legs, have some coffee, whatever. The inside of the station cabin wasn't made to hold a stagecoach full of passengers all at one time. Four men sat around a table built for six at the most. They sat on benches, two men to a side.

"This here's Devlin Jacobsen. He's Indian Agent over to Fort Defiance," Fred said.

I nodded at them.

Fred didn't introduce the soldiers, a captain and two from the ranks, a sergeant and a buck private.

"Mr. Owens," the agent said. "We have information that you have shot two Navajos to death. We'll need to take you back to Fort Defiance with us."

"Won't work," I said.

"What won't work?"

"Neither you nor the army has jurisdiction over

43

Apache County. You can't legally take me to the fort."

The agent puffed up, all indignant. "You murdered two Navajos."

"Ain't no law in Apache County or in all Arizona that would find me guilty. Pure self-defense."

"Captain McElroy. Arrest that man!"

I held up my hand. The room went quiet. "Mr. Agent Man, do you know why I went onto tribal land? I trailed three Wells Fargo horses north. I found them bunched up with a herd of Indian ponies. I took those three Fargo horses back. Now. Are you familiar with what happens to horse thieves? They get strung up, hanged by the neck until dead."

The agent sputtered. "Indians always take horses. It's part of their culture."

"Teach 'em different, then. Because if they steal Wells Fargo horses, I'll come riding. And if they shoot at me, they'd better not miss, because once I've been shot at, the shooter is a dead man. That's self-defense. You've got no grounds for taking me to Fort Defiance." I turned to go.

"Then you admit killing the Navajos, one a young boy."

"Like I said, pure self-defense." I left the room.

Navajos did a lot of shooting at me over the years, and I shot back some. They missed. I didn't. And somewhere along the line, they began to figure it wasn't their bad shooting to blame, there was something strange about me. It wasn't that they missed every time they pulled a trigger, it was their bullets bouncing off me like I was made of iron or going right through me like I was a ghost of some kind. So among the Navajo, I became known as Iron Man by some and Ghost Man by others.

It's not that I particularly dislike Navajos, it's that I can't abide a man taking another man's belongings without so much as a "by your leave." God gave us ten commandments and that's not too many for a man to keep. I figure a man stays within those ten and he'll never get crosswise of the law. One of the ten is—thou shalt not steal.

Part II

Outlaw Heaven

Commodore Perry Owens stood up from the table. "Young'un, it's getting down to time I gotta keep my eye on the store."

"Store?"

"Yeah. Right here in the store."

I have no idea why he called the Bucket of Blood a store, but I knew there was much left to the story of Commodore Perry Owens. "May I come again tomorrow? I'm sure there's much more we need to talk about."

Commodore's eyes twinkled with humor. "Sure enough. Come in the morning. Not too early. You can eat from the free lunch, if you want."

I gathered my pens and foolscap tablet, stored them away in my leather bag, and stood. Commodore thrust out his hand. I took it. He gave my hand one shake and released it. "Tomorrow morning, then," I said.

"Be a pleasure. Surely will."

He saw me past the bar and stood still until I was through the batwings. He didn't suggest anywhere a young reporter could stay, but I'd heard that the Havasu House was good, and I went to find out if it was.

• • •

I stood at the front door of the Bucket of Blood. My pocket watch showed three minutes to ten in the morning. Two doors were swung closed from outside the batwings. They were locked. There was no bell or knocker on the doors. All I could do was wait. I wondered for a spilt second if Commodore was telling me he didn't want to talk to me anymore.

"Mornin'," Commodore said. He'd turned onto the boardwalk in front of the Bucket of Blood from a side street. "Bit early, ain't ya?" Again, there was humor in his eyes, but his face was stone somber. I got the feeling Commodore Perry Owens didn't smile with his face very often.

"I'm eager to hear more of what you have to say, C.P. Perhaps that eagerness put speed into my steps."

"How'd it go at the Havasu House?"

Does Commodore know everything that goes on in this burg? "Seems a good establishment. I left my paraphernalia there. I won't catch today's train, considering the years we have yet to cover."

"Well, then, come on in." Commodore rapped on the closed doors with the head of the cane he carried. In moments, the doors swung open, and the barman said, "Early, are you, C.P.?"

"The youngster—" he waved at me with his

48

cane, "—still has things to talk about with me."
He shouldered his way through the batwings, and
I followed.

"Same place as yesterday," Commodore said.
"Hey, Frick. Got any coffee for an old cowboy?"

"Always got coffee, C.P., the place runs on
coffee, ya know."

"Cuppa java, if you please, then. How 'bout
you?" he said to me.

I nodded. Coffee would start the day with Commodore well. I didn't mention the sunny-side-up
eggs and fried potatoes and thick-sliced bacon
and breakfast rolls smeared with apple butter
that I'd had for breakfast at the Havasu House.
After all, I'd eaten before seven and here it was
pushing ten thirty. Coffee'd be very good. And it
was.

"Where'd we leave off?" Commodore said.

"You were telling me about Navajos stealing
horses. Was that a big problem?"

"Not really. They'd make off with a few head
and I'd have to get the critters back, but Navajos
raise sheep. One man on foot can herd a lot of
sheep. When it came to losing horses, more'n
likely white men was to blame."

"Is that so? You mean there were many bad
men on the prowl back then?"

"Young feller, you would not believe."

"I suppose the West was really wild in those
days."

A car backfired outside and Commodore's hand went to his cane. His sharp gaze fastened on the batwing doors. After a moment, he relaxed and lifted his coffee mug. He looked at me as he sipped at the coal-black brew. "You'll need to remember . . . well, you're too young to remember, but those were the days when ranges in Texas were overgrazed and all that belly-high grass on the Colorado Plateau looked like the answer to a lot of problems, cattle problems, I mean."

I must have looked puzzled, because Commodore put his cup down and placed his hands on the table, palms down. "You see, the A and P got all the way to Canyon Diablo in '81. Government gave the railways every other section of land for forty miles on either side of the tracks. So the A and P had lots of real estate to sell. That's what financed them."

"OK, but what's that got to do with white men stealing cows and horses?"

"Just you wait, youngster. Give me time to explain it all to you."

"Sorry." I drained my coffee cup. Commodore filled it up again from the pot on the table.

"So, with grass in Texas gone short and too many people crowding in, outfits like the Hash-knife and the Twenty-Four came into Arizona. Figure this, youngster. The Aztec Land and Cattle Company alone shipped forty thousand cows as far as Holbrook on the A and P, and turned 'em loose south of the tracks."

"That's the Hashknife Outfit, right?"

"It is. And forty thousand cows on what looks like free range, along with some fifteen thousand wearing the Twenty-Four brand, and a bunch of little outfits like the Z Bar and Henry Huning's ranch and Stott's place, and you're tempting every bad man riding the outlaw trail."

"Where did that leave you, then?" I asked.

"Me? I concentrated on raising good horses and keeping my nose clean."

"Any special techniques you used?" My questions came without my thinking much about them, and I wrote Commodore's answers and comments down in shorthand as he spoke.

"I learned a couple of good tricks from Zack Decker. He was a Mormon who lived in Taylor but had a ranch of sorts over by Cottonwood Wash."

"A Mormon that did tricks?"

"Kinda. He went a bit out of his way to show folks that he always shot straight and true, and that he could get his gun, handgun or long gun, into action while other folks were still scratching their heads, wondering what to do."

"I've heard that you were always ready to shoot up a tin can."

"I was. The Clantons moved up from Tombstone after that shootout with the Earps and Doc

Holliday, setting up a Seventy-Four ranch in Alma, New Mexico. Easy to change a 24 to a 74, don't you reckon? Gus Snider ran a bunch of outlaws over to Round Valley. The Blevins bunch had what they called a ranch on Cherry Creek. And there was a plenty of footloose cowboys willing to make ends meet by shooing off a cow or two or a dozen here and there, or take a team of horses, and what not."

"Did anyone steal any of your horses?"

"No one that lived to tell the tale."

I couldn't think of a follow-up question to that comment, so I drank a big swallow of the Bucket of Blood's horseshoe-floating coffee.

1

"Hello, the fire." I let the cowboys know I was coming in.

"Hello, yerself. Who are ya, 'n waddaya want?"

"No need to get your back up, Hamp. It's me. Commodore Owens."

"Oh."

I heard hammers being released, but I had no way of knowing if all were.

"Come on in. Coffee's hot."

I got off Morg while I was still outside the circle of light thrown by the fire. I ground-tied Morg. "Comin' in," I said. I carried my coffee cup in my left hand.

Four cowboys were hunkered on their heels around a little fire. Old Man Blevins, Hamp and John Blevins, and another brother who went by the name of Andy Cooper. Someone told me he was wanted for killing a man down in Texas.

They knew me and I knew them by sight. But I was there for another reason. I was hunting missing Z Bar beef, and their trail passed close by.

" 'Preciate the coffee," I said.

Hamp Blevins poured. "What brings you out toward the Rim?"

"Someone's driving a dozen or so head of Z Bar stock over this way. I'm out to show them the evil of their ways."

"Ain't us," Andy Cooper said.

"Know that, Andy. If it were you, I'd not walk up to your fire with a coffee cup in my hand."

"Hmph," Andy snorted.

"I was wondering, Andy. Wondering if any of you Blevins boys would like to ride along. Come along and help me get our cows back."

The Blevins boys all studied their coffee cups like they could read the future in the grounds left in the bottoms. No one volunteered.

"Well, thanks a bunch for the coffee," I said. I tossed the dregs out, tapped the cup a couple of times with my other hand, and started to go back to where Morg stood waiting.

Young Andy Cooper half-hollered, "Hey, Commodore."

I turned to face him.

"I'd admire to ride with ya."

I nodded. "Good. Saddle up. I'll wait."

Andy Cooper rode hard and he didn't talk a lot, which suited me fine, because I don't talk much myself. We found the cows on a broad stretch of flat land just north of Show Low Creek. They were bunched up in a corral and some cowboys were heating running irons in a little juniper stick fire. I took my Winchester '76 from its scabbard and rode with it across my saddle bows. Andy did the same. I kept the corral between us and the branding-iron fire. I motioned Andy to go round the other side, which he did. Two cowboys rustled around with the fire.

"Iron's 'bout hot 'nough," the one with the floppy hat said.

"Denny, I been thinkin'," the other one said.

"Don't think too much, 'r yer hair'll catch fire from the heat."

"Denny, I'm wondering."

"Whacha wondering?"

"We ain't got no lariat. How we gonna ketch them cows? How we gonna change them Z Bar brands?"

Me and Morg just snuck right up to the corner of the corral, and I could just make out Andy on the other side. I jacked a shell into the chamber of my Winchester. Things got real quiet. Denny and the kid with him just froze.

"Mister." The kid's voice was just above a whisper. "Mister?"

"You all got a bunch of Z Bar cows in this here corral," I said. "Could it be you's figuring on making the Z Bar brands into something else? A eight cross, maybe? Huh?"

Andy jacked a shell into his rifle, and the kid started sniffling.

I used the name the kid had said. "Denny. What you got to say about all this?"

It was getting on toward sunset, but I could

make out Denny's shrug. "You know what happens to rustlers?" I said.

Again he shrugged.

"How come you got my outfit's cows, then?"

The weeping kid stopped bawling and said, "Uncle Bart. It were Uncle Bart. He promised us two dollars a head if we'd get him some cows."

"Uncle Bart?"

"That'll be Bart Bigelow," Andy said. "I know where he camps out. Like as not he's at the dugout he made down on Silver Creek."

"That right, Denny?" I swung the muzzle of my Winchester over so it pointed right at him. "That right?"

Denny shrugged.

"Horses coming," Andy said.

"I hear 'em." I dismounted and shooed Morg off toward the creek.

A rifle fired and Andy let out a curse. "Too damned close," he said, and jumped off the far side of his horse.

Four riders pounded toward us from the east, raising a cloud of dust and firing like they had all the bullets in the world. I took a bead on the lead horse, a three-color paint, and squeezed off a shot. The horse went down and the rider tumbled head over heels to the ground. When he scrambled to his feet, I put him down again with a shot in the brisket. I jacked another shell into my Winchester.

I switched my aim to another rider, not worrying about the one I'd shot. He was dead.

The other three scattered. There wasn't all that much cover on the flat, but they ran for what there was. Andy was firing, but the running horses showed that his lead took little effect.

"Aim for the horses," I hollered.

A six-gun cracked and a bullet plowed into the dirt not an inch from my left foot. I whirled and pulled the trigger when the Winchester's muzzle lined up with Denny, whose hand worked at earing back the hammer of an old Colt Army M1861. My bullet took him just above the belt buckle and knocked him on his butt, where he sat, staring with disbelieving eyes at the blood stain spreading on his shirt.

"They're running, Commodore," Andy hollered.

A glance showed me that the other three bad-men were almost to the juniper treeline. I shouldered my M1876 and shot as fast as I could work the lever. My bullets took two of the running men between the shoulder blades and they dropped, lifeless. The third one jagged just as I pulled the trigger and my bullet smashed into the joint of his left shoulder. He hit the ground howling, and I figured his wound wasn't mortal. Not right away anyways.

"Jeez," Andy said. "I heard you could shoot, but I never seen the likes."

"Man who steals another man's beef deserves to get shot."

"But jeez. Them fellers is a good hunnert yards off."

"I'd a hit 'em at a quarter of a mile if I had a clear shot."

"Jeez."

"Come on. We got cows to take back to the Z Bar."

The kid was still sobbing. Denny looked to be on his last legs, so to speak. A gut-shot man don't often live, unless he can get to Doc Goodfellow, who's way down in Tucson. I whistled, and in a minute, Morg came looking for a treat, like I taught him.

"Come on, Andy. Let's go get that shoulder-shot jehu."

"He can still shoot," Andy said. He sounded nervous.

"If he tries, I'll kill him." I put my one-in-a-thousand '76 into its saddle scabbard and pulled my Remington, checked it, and put it away. I started for the wounded man. After a minute, Andy came along.

We got the shoulder-shot man back to the corral where Denny was crying and calling for his ma. I'd taken the shirts off the two dead men and we used them to bandage up the shoulder wound. I never asked his name. "Boy," I said, "Doc Woolford over to Show Low's a good sawbones.

Either you and this man ride over there, or you ride by yourself and fetch him. Me and Andy Cooper're gonna take these cows back to where they belong."

"Who are you, mister?"

"Commodore Perry Owens," I said.

2

A man has to be careful about where he practices shooting. Off out on the range, it's not likely, but a lead bullet from a .44, pistol or rifle, can travel a good mile and still make a man-sized hole in anything it hits, man or beast. Wouldn't do to have someone or some thing hit by a practice bullet. So often as not, I go down to Lithodendron Wash, 'cause its walls are high enough so a bullet ain't likely to fly over 'em and soft enough so's the bullet plows in rather than ricocheting off to God only knows where.

Fine day in September, if I remember right, and I was riding a lineback buckskin that I naturally called Buck. I'd got me a buckskin mare with some thoroughbred in her and Jim Houck's pa had a buckskin quarterhorse stud. I figured the two would throw a good colt, and I was right. Buck had the long legs of his ma and the black points and lined back of his pa. He was about as smart as a horse comes, and had more than enough bottom to get a man from St. Johns to Holbrook without breaking his wind. So I ran him from my place on Cottonwood Seep to where you drop off into Lithodendron Wash from the south. Just as we were about to scramble down the side of the wash, the sound of pistol fire came from a little further east. We went down the incline careful, without raising a big cloud of dust. Then Buck, he catfooted up the wash, stepping in the sand that accumulated where the water ran of a rainstorm so there was no click of hoof against stone. Smart horse, that Buck. Almost wished he'd not lost his balls as a yearling.

The sound of careful shooting came from ahead, just beyond the bend that took Lithodendron's channel in a sharp turn north. We rode around the corner and stopped to watch a young man, probably no more than fifteen or sixteen years old, practice his draw and shoot.

The boy stood square to his target, an old fencepost stood up against a niche in the east bank, about fifty feet away. His hand went to the Colt's Peacemaker at his hip. He drew fast and smooth, but not rushed, and when the Peacemaker's barrel came level, he touched off a round. The bullet smashed into the middle of the target post. He'd of gutshot a man at that same distance.

Without turning, he replaced his pistol. "I reckon you'll be Commodore Perry Owens," he said. He drew and fired again, putting lead within half an inch of the first hit.

"I am."

"I ain't done nothing."

"Guilty conscience?"

"No. But I'm after the man what killed my brothers. If he's around, I'll find him."

"Ain't you a bit young to be riding after revenge?"

The boy drew a third time and put the bullet right between the first two. He nodded. "Probably. But a Peacemaker don't care about my age as long as I pull the trigger right and send the lead where it's meant to go."

"A man could put it that way, I reckon. If you don't mind, and I'm not trying to pry into your affairs, ya know, but if you don't mind, I'd admire to know your name."

"Ruel Gatlin."

"A Colorado Gatlin?"

"Yep."

"Brother to them boys what got shot over to Telluride, then?"

"Yep."

"What brings you to Arizona?"

"Hunting a man, like I said."

I put a question mark on my face.

"Johnny Havelock. 'Cept nowadays folks call him Ness."

"Know him. Some say he rides the Outlaw Trail." Then I remembered something I'd heard. "Say. Didn't I hear that Ness Havelock was bushwhacked in Moab the other night? Heard he's buried right there in Moab's graveyard."

"Something's buried there. Can't believe Ness

Havelock'd fall for that kind of bushwhacking, though."

"Garet Havelock's got a spread down south toward Silver Creek. If Ness's in the country, sooner or later, he'll turn up there. And I hear that the shooting scrape in Telluride was on the up and up, no bushwhacking, no back shooting, just a straight up shootout, and Havelock came out on top."

The boy drew and fired, putting another bullet alongside the others. He replaced the Peacemaker, then repeated the process.

He flipped open the loading gate and started ejecting his spent brass.

"Mind if I take a shot or two at your target?"

He shrugged.

I stepped off Buck and ground-tied him. Times like this take a little showing off. If a man shoots unusual good at a target, not often someone who's watched that shooting will draw on him at a later time.

I drew my Remington Army as I walked past Gatlin and triggered it as my right foot came down solid on the ground. I thumbed the hammer back as I took two steps forward and pulled the trigger when my right foot was down solid again. After the fourth shot, I holstered the Remington, turned around, and walked back to where Gatlin stood, gun loaded, waiting for me to get out of the way.

"Reckon the stories are true, then," Gatlin said.

"Stories?"

"They say Commodore Owens is a heller with a gun and it don't pay to go up against him."

"Is that what they say?"

He pointed at the target post. My four bullets hit a good six inches above the place where Gatlin's had chewed away a good part of the target's belly. I could have covered the place my bullets hit with the palm of my hand, easy.

"A man should hit what he shoots at," I said, "work or play."

"My brother Lawrence always said you should have both feet on the ground to shoot."

"Surest way."

"But you was walking."

I nodded. "Flusters the man who wants to shoot you if you keep moving. Like you favor one hand over the other—I prefer to shoot with my right hand—you favor one leg over the other, too. When that foot is connected solid with the ground, you're as good as stopped, and that's when you touch off a round. Wanna try it?"

"You bet I do."

So I spent the better part of a hour helping young Gatlin get to be as accurate with shooting at a walk as he was standing still.

He reloaded his Peacemaker and shoved it into its holster. "Outta cartridges," he said. "I'll keep the five in my six-gun. A man never knows who he'll run into."

I nodded. "Good thinking. Don't reckon anyone's gonna sneak up on your blind side."

"Thank you for the pointers, Commodore."

"More than welcome. And Ruel, if you don't mind me calling you that, you might think twice about trying to gun down Havelock. He's a good man, a hard man, but a good one. He don't go around starting fights, but he finishes them when they get started."

"He killed my brothers. They won't rest easy until he's dead."

"All I'm asking you to do is think about it. Just sit and think."

"Been doing nothin' but think about shooting Ness Havelock since I left Telluride."

I made no more comments. I'd had my say, and I knew Ruel Gatlin would come out second best if he braced Ness Havelock. But I wasn't wearing no kind of a badge, and words carry only so much weight.

We rode to Holbrook together, left our horses at Brown and Kinders livery stable. I went to Aunt Hattie's for the first meal since I left my place at dawn. Gatlin stopped off at the Bucket of Blood, but I don't think he had much drinking on his mind.

People are bound to ask him what he was doing with Commodore Owens, and he'll tell them.

Ruel Gatlin ain't a man of many words, so he'll tell it clean and sparse and maybe another fable will grow and people will refrain from drawing guns against me just because of a story they heard.

Anyway, I can hope it works that way. I can purely hope.

3

My homestead, which got me water rights to Cottonwood Seep and virtual rights to graze my stock anywhere south of the A&P tracks, made me next-door neighbor to the Zeigler outfit, Houck's ranch, and others that lay to the west. As I was the only cowboy on my spread, I didn't run many cattle; I concentrated on horses.

They say Apache County was outlaw heaven in those days, and I suppose it was. But the biggest lawbreakers of all was the outfit they called the St. Johns Ring—the power mongers of Apache County.

At the center of the Ring stood Solomon Barth. It was him, in fact, that convinced the territorial legislature to carve off a hunk of Yavapai County and turn it into Apache County. And he got the county seat assigned to St. Johns. Almost every political officer in the county was a member of the St. Johns Ring. It was like this. Albert J. Banta, the man who helped Barth get Apache County set up, was both probate judge and district attorney. Later C. L. Gutterson took over the DA job. A Mexican named Tony Perez was the first sheriff. A lot of good he did. He was crooked as a dog's hind leg, and J. L. Hubbell, the trading post owner that followed Perez, was no better. A man would wonder how in the world a sheriff could be fair and straight about upholding the law when he made so much money from trading whiskey and rifles to the Indians. Didn't make sense then, don't now. Even the St. Johns Herald was part of the Ring. No choice, I reckon. Sol Barth put up most of the money to get that paper up and going.

Dave Udall told me one day, he said, "Damn. We've got a lot of Mormons in this county, but we can't get a single office away from that St. Johns Ring. They use deceit, fraud, ballot box stuffing, vote miscounting, and forcibly preventing our people from voting . . . they'll do anything short of murder to keep their people in office."

Those of us what ran livestock found ourselves on the other side of the fence from the Ring. Sometimes I wondered if those people didn't get a share of the cows and horses run off and sold by the outlaw element. People began coming to me when stock got rustled because I'd go out and get them cows back. Horses were more difficult. Basically, it was Barth, county officers, businessmen, and Mexican sheepmen on one side; Mormons, ranchers, and cowboys on the other.

Let me tell you how it was. Here's one example. It happened after the hullabaloo between cowboys and Mexicans at a fiesta in St. Johns.

Dick Greer had a run-in with a Mexican sheepherder out on the range and ended up killing him.

Now Tony Perez had deputized about eighty Mexicans. You saw a Mexican on the streets and chances were that he was one of those deputies. Greer figured he'd get no kind of fair break from the Mexican law, so he gave himself up to the judge in Holbrook. But those Mexican deputies nabbed Joe Woods, a Greer cowboy, along with a black rider they called "Nigger Jeff," and locked 'em up. Only they never put 'em in jail, their lockup was Sol Garth's hotel.

That's when Nat Greer, Dick's brother, came to Cottonwood Seep, asking me for help. I owed Dick a favor or two, and he'd always been stand-up honest with me, so I said I'd do what I could.

Nat's horse was fairly well rode out by the time he got to my place, it being a good thirty miles from St. Johns.

"We'd best be on our way," I said, after I heard what he had to say. "I know most of them Mexes, and they know me. Let's go talk to them."

I had Morg and Buck in the corral by my cabin. I saddled Morg and Nat switched his tack from his blaze-faced brown to my buckskin. We took off lickety-split for the Garth Hotel in St. Johns.

After we crossed the Zuni River, Nat split off and rode to bring more guns. By the time I got to the first Mexican adobes on the lower flat next to the Little Colorado, Nat was there with six of his cowboys, armed with six-guns and Winchesters.

"You men hang back right now," I said. "Let's not have a shootout if we can do this thing without gunfire."

"Sunzabitches got Joe 'n Jeff," Greer said. "No telling what they'll do to 'em."

"I'll go have a look. Let's see what happens." I took out the Colt Peacemaker I'd put on for the ride and added a .45 caliber cartridge to the cylinder. I spun it to make sure everything moved smooth. I went off down the street until I was in plain sight of the Barth Hotel.

"Commodore," Greer called. "Don't you go get yourself shot before we can do anything."

I could see a bunch of Mexicans all over and around the hotel. I took off my hat and ran my fingers through my long hair—purposefully growed long so any Indian who could take my scalp would have a fine trophy—spreading it out across my shoulders. In those days, my hair hung halfway to my belt, so I let the Mexes have a good look at who was coming. I drew the Colt Peacemaker and held it alongside my leg as I walked the thirty yards from where Morg was tied and Greer and his cowboys sat their horses with Winchesters at hand.

"Perez! Commodore Owens here. I'm coming in."

No answer.

I just kept on walking. No boardwalk in front of the hotel. Nowhere for a gunman to hide, really.

70

Just a bunch of Mexicans with rifles and pistols standing there. Some I knew by sight. Others I didn't. Made no difference. My Peacemaker wasn't even cocked.

The closer I got, the quieter they got. No one made any kind of a move, because they'd all heard of how I could plug a two-bit piece dead center from twenty-five or thirty feet away, and a man's forehead is quite a bit bigger than a two-bit piece.

Some of them was muttering something in Mexican, but I walked on by like they wasn't even standing there. Those around the door stepped aside without me even having to tell them to. I opened the door with my left hand. "Perez. I'm coming in," I said.

I did, but Tony Perez weren't there. And he'd deputized so many people that there weren't near enough badges for 'em. Besides, none a them was gonna try to arrest me anyway.

Joe and Jeff sat in overstuffed chairs like they was checked into the hotel.

"By all that's holy. You two are the laziest cowpokes I ever saw. Nat's waiting for you to get to work. So you just traipse on down the street. Hear?"

They stood up all meek and cowed.

"Go on. Ain't nobody gonna stop ya. Dick's at the judge's place in Holbrook. He's the one in trouble, if there is any. Ain't right for you two to be held for something you never done. Now let's go."

No Mexican made no kind of suspicious move, because none wanted to get drilled. And I would of drilled anyone who tried.

Mind you, I wasn't no lawman, but more and more people come to me when there was trouble or when someone was breaking the law.

It's like this. Tony Perez just plain didn't like Anglos. He got in with Sol Barth and the St. Johns Ring because Barth's wife were Mex. Even the newspaper, which was indebted to the Ring, wrote that "Mr. Perez's own deputies represent the greatest criminals in the country." So when a white man or a Mormon got stock stole, there was no way in hell that Perez or any of his deputies would follow up on it. Might even a been that they was in on the rustling from the get-go.

Perez lost the next election and Juan Lorenzo Hubbell took his place. And if you think Tony was a mess, J.L. put him to shame. It seemed that those were the days when the sheriff and his deputies were more interested in lucre than in criminals. Bad men flooded the territory, coming up from Texas and across from New Mexico, but there might as well have been no law as far as the outlaws were concerned.

Oz Flake and Sam Brown and Frank Wattron converged on my little horse ranch in September of '86.

"Light and set," I hollered when I seen who was coming. "Y'all're a bit off the beaten path, ain't ya?"

"Any coffee?" Frank said.

"Always got some. May be a bit strong, though."

"Don't matter."

They dismounted and crowded into my little dugout cabin.

"Gol. This place needs a woman's touch," Oz said.

"You ought to know." I smiled to take the sting out of what I said. "You got enough women around your place to do for all of us."

"C.P., this is serious," Sam said. He sipped at the hot coffee I gave him. "Sheesh. This mud'd melt a horseshoe for sure."

"What's serious, Sam?"

"Us. Me and Frank and the people in Holbrook and Snowflake and the rest of the Mormon towns, Oz says. Oh, and the Apache County Stock Growers Association, we all agree."

"That's good. What is it you all agreed on?"

"Commodore Perry Owens. We want you to run for Apache County sheriff."

Part III

Rule of Law

By ten in the morning, C. P. Owens and I were seated in the Bucket of Blood sipping coffee. Actually, I'd begun my third day in Seligman with a hearty breakfast at the Havasu House, bolstered by some delightful conversation with Betty McNeil, one of the Harvey Girls at the hotel.

"You're in good spirits, young man," Commodore said. As usual the humor was in his eyes, not on his face.

"I should be. I'm about to hear what happened in Apache County after Commodore Perry Owens became sheriff. That's something for a news hound to be happy about."

"You ain't no hound. You're hardly more than a puppy."

I grinned, but said nothing.

"Well, where were we?"

I read from my notes. "Oz Flake, Frank Wattron, and Sam Brown asked you to run for sheriff of Apache County."

"They did."

"And you did. Run for sheriff, I mean."

Commodore nodded. "Outlaws had to be taken care of. Too many bad men'd come into the county and store men like J. L. Hubbell, and Mex sheepherders like Tony Perez never had the gumption to get the job done."

"Did you have experience for the job? Ever been a lawman before?"

"Never."

"Then why did people think you could do the job?"

"I never lie. I never cheat. I never brag. I don't stand around talking about what I'm gonna do, I just do it. And everyone knew I never asked to be sheriff. I said I'd do it if everyone wanted me to, but I didn't stand up and wave my hat and go on about what great things I'd do, and all that."

"I heard you could hit tin cans on a fence from a galloping horse."

"I can."

"And you could hit a one-by-twelve set edge-wise, using a pistol in each hand."

"I could."

"So your shooting got you elected, then."

Commodore chuckled. "Sam Brown and Frank Wattron got me elected."

"Many men were good with a gun back then. Were you better than them? Is that why you got voted in?"

"Probably not."

"Then why?"

"I was good all right, but more than that, I didn't owe nobody nothing."

"You were not in debt, then?"

"Well, I didn't owe any money, that's true, but I didn't have connections that would make me be unfair, like Hubbell did with that Humphreys outlaw who ran with the Clanton bunch. He let that rowdy go because he was married to a sister of Hubbell's wife. I was single. My homestead was free and clear. My horses were top notch. And I never took guff from no man."

"Then what was the very first thing you did after getting elected?"

"It wasn't me, but they held a grand ball to celebrate the election."

"Who did you dance with? Anyone in particular?"

"Don't dance."

The surprise must have shown on my face.

Humor came to Commodore's eyes again. "Here I am, a saloon owner and a former gunman, and I don't drink. I don't smoke. I don't pander with doves. And I don't dance. Joe McKinney did enough dancing for the two of us. At least he claimed he did."

"But you're not a Mormon."

"I was raised a Quaker. Lots of what Quakers teach strikes me as being right. So that's what I do. Or don't do."

"And what was the second thing you did after being elected?"

"That's a stickler. Once elected, I had to post a bond."

"A bond? As if you were going to escape, like a common criminal?"

"In those days, the county sheriff collected tax money from them what owed it. I was required to post that bond to ensure me against all that money."

I'd not known about sheriffs posting bonds, so I decided to dig a little more. "Just how much were you required to post?"

"Ten thousand."

"What!" I did some quick calculation. "That's as much as a dozen men might make in a year."

Commodore nodded. "And that's not all. I had to get sureties from three people who was worth, all put together, more than the bond."

"Did Frank Wattron and Samuel Brown do the sureties? They're the ones who talked you into running."

Commodore gave a little negative shake of his head. "No. It were those two Englishmen, Smith and Carson, who owned the Twenty-Four Land and Cattle Company, and the Dutchman Henry Huning from over Show Low way."

"Then you owed those people."

"I did, but I never give a damn, pardon the language, whether I was sheriff or not. So I didn't have to sidle up to no one's warm side to stay in office. That Twenty-Four, and Oz Flake and Hank Huning and other smaller outfits needed to get the thievery stopped. That was my job. Part of it, at least."

"Sounds like a very big job. But what did you do between the election—when was that? November '86?"

"Yes. A cold November it was, too. Didn't snow on election day, but there was a foot on the ground a couple of days later."

"Does becoming a sheriff require a great deal of preparation?"

"I clean my weapons every day anyway, so that was taken care of. Gus Ziegler and Jim Houck said they'd watch after my stock, so that was no problem. Joe McKinney said he'd be my deputy, and him and me moved to St. Johns at the end of December. I got a room at McCormick's boarding house and Joe got one at Barth's Hotel. It was cold, and I figure Hell was froze over on the first day of January, eighteen and eighty-seven, but me and Joe was ready for whatever come, mostly."

1

They swore me in on Monday the 3rd of January. The 1st is a holiday and the 2nd fell on the Sabbath. I put my hand on the Bible and I swore to uphold the constitution of USA, the laws of the Territory of Arizona and of Apache County, so help me God. And I meant it.

"Good to have you for sheriff," Ernie Tee said. He picked up a sheaf of papers, straightened them out, and handed them to me. "Warrants. Some from Prescott. We have no doubt but that you'll serve those warrants. All of them."

I didn't say yes, didn't say no. But I took the warrants. "Is that all?"

"It is. We're looking forward to results, C.P. This county needs to settle down."

"I'll get to work, then," I said, and took leave of the county supervisors, just left them sitting there chewing their cuds. I knew some were beholden to Sol Barth and the St. Johns Ring, but all I could do was to serve the warrants and arrest those who'd broke the law. I must say I wasn't in a very good mood when I got to the sheriff's office in the back of the redrock courthouse.

"You look like a storm blowin' in," Joe McKinney said when I came through the door. I just waved that handful of bench warrants at him.

"What's that?"

"Work." I handed him the warrants and sat down at the desk. From the looks of things, it would take me the better part of a month to get the desk straightened out so I knew where what was. The county supervisors'd given me a badge, but not one for Joe. I started through the desk, looking for deputy badges. I found them, all four of them, under the wanted flyers in the bottom righthand drawer.

"Joe." When he looked up, I tossed him a badge. "Raise your right hand."

He did.

"Do you swear to uphold the laws of the U.S. of A., the Territory of Arizona, and Apache County, so help you God?"

"I do," Joe said, and he became my first deputy sheriff. He pinned the badge to his vest. Rustling the sheaf of warrants, he said, "You look at these, C.P.?"

"Not yet."

"Old as the hills, some of them."

"Who we gotta catch?"

"Lee Renfro, for one."

"People die when Lee's around. You heard where he is?"

"Nope. Ain't heard that he's left the country, either."

"Who else."

"Lot Smith." Joe looked at me.

I shrugged.

"Phin and Ike Clanton."

"Makes a man wish the Earps had finished their job, don't it?" Hank Smith and Tom Carson of the Twenty-Four Land and Cattle Company had ensured me. At the same time, they made sure I knew that the Clantons' 74 cows had twins most years and sometimes triplets. They made sure I knew that brand-changing had to stop.

"George and Bill Graham."

"What for?"

"Suspicion of robbing a stage."

"They never did." People under the gun see visions, I'd come to think. Witnesses may have been on the spot, but rarely do they remember things as they really happened. That's been my experience anyway.

"Kid Swingle."

"That boy'll end up in Yuma."

"Long Hair Williams."

"My hair ain't long no more. Should be easy to tell the difference."

"One here for Jack Diamond, you know. That's what Billy Evans likes people to call him."

"Jack Diamond?"

"His lucky card, he says."

"What for?"

"Assault with a deadly weapon."

"That little squirt?"

"Says so here."

"Arrest him if you run across him. Most likely in a poker game in Winslow or Holbrook. Judge'll probably fine 'im and let 'im go."

Joe gave me a hard look before he read the last name. He knew about me and Andy and the rustler fight on the bench north of Show Low Creek. "C.P., there's one here on Andy Cooper— Andrew Arnold Blevins. It's two years old."

I almost said damn, but swearing don't get a man nowhere. "What for?"

"Stealing stock."

"Andy?"

"Says so here."

"I told that boy to be careful. Once there's a warrant out, the law can kill a man for looking cross-eyed. They just call it 'Resisting arrest.' You'd better give me that warrant."

Joe handed it to me.

"What? Navajo horses? They're forever running off with ours. Andy was probably just returning the favor." I folded the warrant and put it in my shirt pocket. "Leave it to me."

We filed the other warrants in the sheriff's desk, and I went to get ready to ride around the county to tell ranch hands and the hangers-on that law had come to Apache County. In fact, I stopped at the Blevins spread on Cherry Creek in hopes Andy'd be there.

I'd camped over on Cottonwood Wash the night before, and jawed with Zach Decker for a while. Him and me see eye to eye on a lot of things.

Took the Cooper warrant out of my pocket and held it out to Zach. "This here warrant is on Andy Cooper. Would you hold it until I come for it?"

He took it. "I can do that." He held the warrant to the fire so he could read it. "Stealing Navajo horses? Don't sound like no crime."

I'd told Zach that if Andy'll stay quiet, this may blow over. And that I was hoping that'd be the case.

Now, I hollered from the front yard. "Hello, the house. Anybody home?"

Hamp Blevins stuck his head out the door. "Whaddaya want?"

"You know, Hamp. I'm sheriff of Apache County now. Don't you guys go pulling no shenanigans while I'm the law and I won't be coming after ya."

Hamp shrugged. Then Andy pushed him out of the way and stepped into the yard. "Howdy, C.P. What brings ya all the way to Cherry Creek?"

"Andy, I got a warrant sitting on my desk . . . a warrant on you."

"I ain't done nothing."

I had to chuckle. "Not sure that's true."

Andy didn't say nothing and he kept his right hand awful close to his six-gun.

"The warrant I got is for Navajo horses. Agent and the army says you stole some."

"I never stole nothing."

"In my book, even if you took ever' horse on Navajo land, it wouldn't be stealing. But the warrant's from the State outta Prescott, pressed by the Indian Agent and the army. So if I get pushed, or if you don't stay outta town when I'm in, I'll have to serve it."

Andy and Hamp never said a thing.

"You hear me, Andy Cooper?"

"Yeah."

"Then you stay outta my way. Like I said, unless I get pushed pretty hard, I'll leave that warrant lie. If you don't stay outta town when I'm there, I'll have to come after you."

"Even if you come, I won't go."

"I know you're stubborn as a mule, kid. But if you act up with me . . . if I've got a reason to come after you, then you'd better come along peaceful. You don't, and I'll have to take you down."

"Don't you try and get tough with me, C.P. I know too much about what all you've been doing."

"I warned you, Andy. You can play it close to the chest and stay out of my way, or you can have me coming after you. Your choice." I reined Morg around and we headed for the Stott place. I had to get the word around. No give for lawbreakers from Commodore Owens. None at all.

2

Sam Brown and Frank Wattron, along with a lot of Mormons and several cattle outfits, got me elected sheriff of Apache County on a law and order ticket, but let me tell you, the job of a sheriff seemed to have precious little to do with finding criminals and socking them away. A sheriff is a lawman, you might say. And that is true. Still, the lion's share of the time of the sheriff of Apache County was spent running around collecting license fees. You heard me right. Collecting license fees. The county supervisors even made it the sheriff's fault if a fee was not collected. They'd assume a man hadn't gone to him what owed the fee and made him fork over. So you know what? I had to pay those delinquent fees out of my own pocket and collect from the skunk who never paid when I could.

Joe McKinney made me a good deputy. I trusted that man from the git-go.

Now. When I took over from J. L. Hubbell, the county jail was more like a pig sty than anything fit for human beings. And Old Jack Conley, the jailer, was fit for little beside tippling the bottle and snoring through his watch. In the end, he let prisoners escape and I fired him. For a while, the jail was empty, but trouble was flaring up all over the county.

A vigilance committee ran down some horse thieves over on the edge of the plateau. The no-goods took three horses, but even one horse stole is enough to get a man hanged.

The three-man committee tracked the horse rustlers to their camp, which was quite well-concealed in a gully down this side of Clear Creek. They must have been awful confident, maybe because they knew I was over to Navajo Springs, the little town that grew up between the stage stop and the railway station on the A&P line. At any rate, the vigilance boys could see the rustlers well from a bluff above their camp. They got off their horses, I mean the vigilance men, lay down, set their long guns on them horse thieves and blasted them.

Two men fell dead. One was Long Hair and the other was Billy Evans. So there was a couple of warrants I didn't have to serve.

I sat in the office for a change, counting and recording the fees I'd collected over the past few days, when Joe McKinney come in.

"By all that's holy," he said through clenched teeth. Then he let out a string of oaths I'd rather not repeat.

"What's wrong?"

"Navajos stole a prime mare from Defiance Cattle Company."

"Guess I'd better saddle up and see if I can get her back."

"Too late."

Joe didn't look happy, to say the least.

"What happened?"

"George Lockhart went after the mare."

"The reservation's outta his jurisdiction. Outta mine, for that matter, but we are the law in the county. You, Me, and Frank."

"They went. Lockhart and two Defiance cowboys named King and Palmer. They never come back."

I stood and took my hat from its peg on the wall. "Sheesh. We'd better go to the agency."

"I been to the agency," Joe said.

I put my hat back and sat down. I reckoned the news wasn't gonna be good. "Lockhart all right?"

Joe shook his head. "Hacked to little pieces outside the hogan of a Navajo name of Hosteen Chee. Chee's dead, too. No tellin' who died first."

"How 'bout the cowboys?"

"Dead. Run and fought for more'n two miles. Shot in the back of the head at close range. No telling what they did to the Navajos."

Joe took a deep breath and let it whoosh out. "Don't like this, C.P., truly don't."

"You left then, right?"

Joe nodded. "Lucky to get out alive. Must a been forty Navajo bucks with rifles all pointing my way. Dogs was chewing on a dead horse.

Reckon it got killed in the fray. The Navajo Hosteen Chee was lying in the hogan, probably pulled in after things died down. Never seen so many mad Navajos in my life."

"Where're the bodies?"

"Got some wagons from Navajo Springs to pick 'em up and haul 'em back."

"Well done." Still, Apache County's my territory and I figured I ought to go talk to the agency and the army. "I'll get over to Fort Defiance first thing."

"I went."

I raised my eyebrows.

"Colonel over there said . . . and I quote . . . 'We'll look into the affair.' "

"I'll bet."

"Yeah. But Chee was dead and someone had to have killed Lockhart and his posse." Joe licked a pair of dry lips. "Me and O.B. and John Scarlett went to Bennet's Trading Post over to Houck's Tank to see if he had any idea who done it."

"He know anything?"

"He said them what did it had already run for the reservation. A bunch of Navajos with scowls on their faces and guns in their hands was hanging around and we could see a bunch more coming. 'Walk your horses away, boys,' I said. They'd a sure come a shootin' if we'd run. But my horse walked something awful slow, almighty slow."

A while later, the army sent me a letter saying Constable Lockhart and "associates" were drunk and were the aggressors in the matter. All the time I was sheriff of Apache County, and later when I was sheriff of Navajo Country, we could never expect the army or the Indian Agent to deliver justice in any form. I'm not saying every white man was in the right, but we surely wasn't in the wrong every time neither.

I'd warned Andy Cooper about his habit of taking other people's stock. And I told him to lay low while I was sheriff. But that boy was forever getting into trouble.

One of his escapades let me get my spurs into the army just a little bit. You see, Andy, his brother, Hamp, and another cowboy from somewhere went up on the reservation and made off with a herd of Navajo horses. The thing about Navajo horses is, they have no brands, at least the horses born and raised Navajo don't. They said Andy and them stole a hundred and three Navajo ponies, and was branding them at a ketch pen over by Canyon Creek. A horde of Navajos descended on the place and started shooting. One bullet caught Hamp Blevins in the hip. The other two cowboys got away, so to speak, and the Indians got all the horses back.

Then the army came.

How they knew I was in Holbrook, I'll never know, but I was talking with Frank Wattron in front of his drug store when a captain and six troopers rode up.

"Sheriff Owens?" the captain said.

"I am."

"I'll be Captain Kerr, J. B. Kerr. I've been detailed with seeking your assistance in the matter of a man called Andy Cooper and his cohorts who stole more than one hundred head of horses belonging to the Navajo people. This man needs to be brought to justice."

I put a finger to the brim of my hat. "Good to know you, Captain. We'd be more than happy to help the army and the agency to apprehend Cooper and his bunch just as soon as you all bring in the Navajo bucks what chopped up Marshal Lockhart and the two men with him. Justice needs to work both ways, Captain. Wouldn't you say?"

The captain hemmed and hawed.

"I've been thinking about mounting a posse to go hunting for them who killed Lockhart, even though I hear they run to New Mexico."

The captain drew himself up in his saddle— he wasn't such a big man to start with and a bit scrawny at that—and said in his best cavalry officer voice, "Surely you know, sir, that bringing a posse onto the Navajo Reservation would put you at odds with the United States Army. We are assigned to guard the rights of the Navajo Nation."

"Are you saying you'd fire on a legal posse led by an elected officer of the law?"

"If it came to that."

"Your troopers up to a firefight? I hear that they've got so much fatigue duty that there's hardly any time for drills."

The captain puffed up. "They are soldiers in the U.S. Army. Of course they can ride and shoot."

"Captain Kerr, I can shoot the head off a turkey at a hundred yards. But then, I spend an hour or two a day practicing. I'm known as a good shot. Just ask around. But I'm by no means the best. Zach Decker is better'n me, and so's Lot Smith. And there's a whole bunch of rannies, including Andy Cooper, who'd stand right behind them two."

The captain got red in the face, but his pistol was in a flap holster and there was no way on God's earth that he could get that weapon out and into action before me and Frank drilled him, and probably his troopers, too.

"You bring me those killers, Captain, and then we'll talk about horse thieves."

"You have no jurisdiction over the Navajo Reservation."

"Lockhart and King and Farmer just went onto Navajo land in hot pursuit of Indians what made off with a prize mare. There wasn't no need for killing."

"They were drunk and disorderly, and started

the shooting themselves. That was our report on the incident."

"If that's how you're gonna treat men who enter the reservation in pursuit of criminals, then we can return the favor when you need us for the same reason. Turn about is surely fair play, Captain. Good day."

I turned to Frank. "I'd be obliged if you've got a can of pine tar, Frank. Don't want none of my horses getting fly blown, ya know."

"Come on in, C.P.," Frank said, and we left the captain and his men on their horses in the street. I bought a can of pine tar, and when I got back to the street, the army was gone. I did hear that Captain Kerr called me a "desperate, determined, and ignorant man." Determined, I am, and at times, desperate. But although I am unschooled, I cannot see where I am ignorant in the least.

3

Becoming sheriff put me at odds with some of the toughest, randiest men in the territory. Men like Lee Renfro and Gus Snider, the Clanton brothers, and the old Mormon enforcer, Lot Smith.

Next to Porter Rockwell, I reckon Lot Smith was an avenging angel, head to foot. He must have known Port Rockwell, because Smith was a bodyguard to Brigham Young when Rockwell was. Never heard of him wearing a badge, though. Still, when I was elected sheriff, Smith was getting along in years, nigh on to sixty, I heard.

I'm not afraid of any man alive, but I don't take chances either. Now Lot Smith. I had a warrant on him for having more than one wife. Some of the Mormons served time in Yuma for that offense, but I kinda figured a man's religion was his own right, and if it caused a man to take care of more than one woman and a herd of youngsters at the same time, then more power to him.

I put the warrant for Lot Smith in a desk drawer and ignored it. Smith's home had originally been at Sunset, up north and west of Winslow. Now I hear he's moved to Tuba City on the reservation.

It weren't often that he'd come all the way down to St. Johns, but one day he was watering his horse at the Little Colorado crossing below the bridge.

"Howdy, Commodore," he said.

" 'Day, Lot. Weather holding for you?"

"Bit dry out in that Tuba City desert, good thing there's a spring or two to irrigate from."

I give him a hard look, taking in the gray streaks in his red hair and full beard. "You take care, Lot," I said.

"I do that always. Somewhere I heard you have a warrant for my arrest. Would you like to serve it right now?" Lot Smith's right hand rested on the butt of the S&W American he had stuffed in his waistband.

"I do. It's in the office. Says something about you having more than one wife."

"Well, that's true." Damned if Lot Smith didn't name every one of his wives, ticking them off with a finger as he did so. "But you don't see no Smith brats in the poor house, do you?"

"County spent more'n two hundred eighty dollars for the poor last quarter," I said.

"Betcha none of the people taking county handouts're Mormon."

"That may be true."

"So. Whatcha gonna do? Drag me in? You'll have to do that over this here Smith and Wesson." He patted the grips of his pistol.

"No, Lot Smith. You kill someone or run off with another man's critters, and you'll see me on your trail. But I don't give a hoot how many wives you have or how many mouths you feed. Deal?"

Lot Smith grinned. "Deal, Commodore." He reined his horse's head out of the creek water. "Come on, Crazy Horse, we got miles to go before dark."

"Tuba?"

"Nah. Stay the night at Oz Flake's place."

"Take care, Lot. Don't let your temper do you in."

"Be seeing ya, Commodore. Right happy to have you as county sheriff. Right happy."

He went north and I went into town. It just wasn't worth the possibility of taking a bullet in the chest just to serve a warrant wrote up out of bigotry.

The brouhaha in Tombstone between the Earps and the Cowboys pushed the Clantons north into Apache County. Old Man Clanton died in an ambush at Guadalupe Canyon and young Billy Clanton went down at OK Corral. Ike and Phin, though, made homestead claims on more than 300 acres of pastureland in Cienega Amarilla, east of Springerville.

From the first, the Clantons were nothing but trouble. They rustled cattle, blotting the Twenty-Four outfit's 24 brand with one they'd registered as 74. They got arrested for burglary, and Ike shot a Mexican through the hip when a Springerville card game got too hot.

Ike Clanton escaped Wyatt's vendetta ride and so far he'd escaped justice in Apache County, but he couldn't escape forever.

The Apache County Stock Growers Association hired a range detective by the name of Jonas Brighton, and gave him the job of apprehending the Clantons. He came to the sheriff's office, looking for help.

" 'Mornin', C.P.," Brighton said at the door.

"Coffee?" I said.

"Don't mind if I do." He come in and took the chair in front of the desk. Bert Miller, one of our deputies, brought Brighton a mug of coffee. He nodded thanks and slugged down half a cup before he said another thing. "C.P., I got good information that says Ike Clanton's down in Black River country. I'd like to find him. Well, that's what the Association's paying me for, but you know I can't arrest him. Need the law to come along. Could you do that, C.P.?"

I had fees to collect and that killer Juan Carillo was waiting for me in Alma, but Bert Miller could go along. "Sorry, Jonas. I can't. Got pressing matters to care for. But Bert can go along. He's a sworn deputy. He can make any arrest, if it comes to that. All right with you, Bert?"

"When ya leaving, Jonas?"

"The sooner, the quicker."

"How long ya figuring on being gone?"

"A week. Ten days, maybe."

"Association paying for grub and cartridges?" I asked.

"It will."

"There you have it, Bert. You get ready and buy your grub and stuff at Schuster's."

"Where'll I meet you then, Jonas?"

"I'll get me a beer at the Monarch while you're getting ready. We'll leave soon as you get your stuff together."

Brighton and Albert Miller rode out just after noon. While the range detective said they'd be gone a week or so, I didn't see them again until after the first of the month, and they'd left on May 14th.

Funny thing was, Phin Clanton was in the county jail when Miller and Brighton come in carrying news of Ike's death. They come into the office on the second of June, while I was working on a report about collecting fees and bringing in Juan Carillo. I laid my pen down. "Find Ike?"

"He ain't gonna cause you no more trouble," Brighton said. "He's dead and buried."

I raised my eyebrow, so Jonas told his story.

He'd gotten word from Hal Simpson that Ike'd been over to Cienega, so him and Miller went there first. Ike Clanton wasn't there. The barkeep at Lonesome Eight said he heard Clanton was headed for Eagle Creek—that word came about the time Jonas and Bert had been out two weeks. Brighton knew Jim Wilson, who had a spread over on Eagle Creek, so they rode in that direction and reached Wilson's place on the night of the 31st. They chawed the fat with Jim for a while and turned in, sleeping on the hay in his barn. Nothing happened.

"Rise 'n' shine, law people," Jim hollered, and Jonas and Bert rolled outta their soogans. Outside, it was still dark.

"Come on in for breakfast when you get the sleep outta your eyes," Jim said. Bert and Jonas headed for the washstand back of Jim's cabin—his little ranch's got all the comforts of home—and washed up. Time Bert and Jonas got into his house, Jim had bacon fried and heaped on a plate in the middle of the table.

"How'd y'all want your eggs?"

"You got eggs?"

"Got some range hens. You're gonna get one egg apiece."

"Sunny-side up," they chorused.

"That was a mighty good breakfast, C.P.," Jonas said to me, "right good."

"So yesterday morning you ate breakfast at Jim Wilson's ranch and today you're telling me Ike Clanton's not gonna bother me no more."

"Hang on, C.P. I'm getting to that part."

He cleared his throat and took a mouthful of coffee. "I heard a horse coming," Bert said, "and

100

when I looked to see who it was, there was Ike Clanton, bigger than life itself, right there in front of the door. I hollered and told him to come peaceful, but he jerked that crazy horse of his around and headed for the brush."

"I had my Colt's drawed," Jonas said, "and when Ike jerked his Winchester outta its boot and laid it on his left arm to take a shot at us, I just naturally plugged him."

"How far off?"

"Twenty yards, maybe."

"One shot?"

"One shot and he fell. Him on one side of the horse, the rifle on the other. We went out to see if we could help him, but he was plumb dead. Shot under one arm and the bullet came out under the other. I reckon it went right through his heart on the way."

"He was plumb dead all right," Bert Miller said. "We buried him as best we could. Jim Wilson had a shovel, but we didn't have no Bible."

"One more warrant I don't have to worry about," I said. "I'll go tell Phin that his brother's dead."

Part IV

Apache County Sheriff

I was getting used to the Havasu House and the folks there, including the Harvey Girls, were getting used to me. As usual, I arrived at the Bucket of Blood with a full stomach, but also with a certain craving for the strong black coffee that seemed to be in inexhaustible supply at C. P. Owens's saloon. C.P. himself sat at our customary table with his customary cup of coffee. I took my customary place and got my foolscap and pen from my leather satchel.

"How's the day treating you, youngster?"

"So far so good, but I reckon it's going to get better."

"How'd you figure that?"

"I figure you're going to tell me about the gunfight in Holbrook where you shot Andy Cooper."

"Read the newspaper. It's still around some-place."

"I'd rather hear it from you."

"You remember what I told Andy Cooper?"

"Stay out of town?"

"What else?"

"You didn't figure taking Navajo horses was a crime."

C.P. smiled with his eyes. "I told him not to stir up trouble as long as I was sheriff and that the warrant would stay buried if he did that."

"I remember that."

"So him and me, we ended up on Holbrook on the same day, with him bragging about killing people. I had no proof on the killings, but I had that warrant, even if it was at Zach Decker's place in Taylor."

"So the gunfight wasn't about the Navajo horses at all, then?"

C.P. shook his head. "It ain't right to kill a man just because he's got skin of a different color or a last name that don't sit right with your own friends. It ain't right. And I figured if I could get Andy into jail, things in Pleasant Valley might simmer down a bit."

"But Andy didn't see it your way?"

C.P. scrubbed a hand across his face. "Andy Cooper never thought any way but his own. I had to shoot him. And, no matter how much I wish I hadn't, I shot that youngster Sam Houston Blevins. Only twelve years old, he was, but the revolver he pointed at me was .45 caliber, and a boy's finger pulls a trigger just as easy as a man's."

"What about Roberts?"

"He was running with a gun in his hand. That

104

meant he had something to hide. Coulda killed him, but I didn't."

I wrote on my foolscap for a minute, thinking about where to point the conversation. C.P. signaled for another cup of coffee.

"Dammit," C.P. said. "Dammit. Didn't want to kill that boy. Purely didn't. But he left me no choice. None at all. After I shot that boy, them newspapermen, them people like you, youngster, they started calling me a killer."

"Why would they do that? Were you?"

C.P. didn't answer right away. He turned his coffee cup around a couple of times, and seemed to watch out the front window as traffic passed. Nowadays, as many horseless carriages went by as carriages or wagons pulled by horses. "Maybe I was. Maybe I was. But that's what was needed at the time."

I took a deep breath and another mouthful of coffee because I was about to ask C.P. a question that might at the least get me thrown out of the Bucket of Blood.

"What's eatin' at you, youngster?"

"Well. Let me see if I can phrase this in a way that will give no offense."

"You want to know how many men I've kilt, don't you?"

A car going by backfired, but neither of us flinched.

"Back then, I'da been out the door with a six-gun in my hand," C.P. said. "Horseless carriages. They'll be the death of more men than a lawman's gun ever was."

"How many, C.P.?"

"Dead? They gotta be dead to be counted as kilt, don't they?"

"If you wish."

"A dozen or so. But that ain't counting Indians or Mexicans."

"Why wouldn't you count them?"

"They ain't Americans. Indians live under a different set of laws. Like I said about George Lockhart. Him a sworn-in lawman and we couldn't get no action from either the agent or the army. So if some Indian makes off with stock from a bona fide owner in Apache County, I'd shoot him outta the saddle, no questions asked. And he'd not be counted as a 'man' in my book."

"Any other exceptions?"

"Mexicans. I don't mean the vaqueros what ride for the Pilar Rancho nor people who've always called this area home. They're Americans to me. Like Tommy Perez. Once a sheriff, always crooked as a dog's hind leg, but I hauled him in. Coulda shot 'im, but I never."

"So. A dozen men dead by your hand, then?"

"Are you listening, youngster? That's what I said, not counting Navajos, who're up north in their own country. And not other country desperado Mexican cow thieves."

"Doesn't sound like enough to earn you the label of killer."

"Well, some of them I wounded died later, like Mose Roberts. But that weren't my fault. T'was the sawbones's fault."

"How many wounded, if I can ask?"

"Fifty-three."

I must have looked surprised, because C.P. chuckled, and that was very uncharacteristic of him. "How many died?" I asked.

"Who knows? I never kept count."

"So you got all the bad men in the county, dead or alive? Is that right?"

C. P. Owens barked a laugh. His eyes swept the customers in the Bucket of Blood. Not many, as it was yet before noon, and Carrie Nation had put the fear of God into men who started drinking in the morning. Drinking at any saloon, for that matter.

"You know, youngster, some of the men called outlaws or bad men or hard men had more gray matter in their skulls than ten men put together."

"Like who?"

"Some run away. Like, I had warrants out for the Graham brothers, George and Bill. Maybe you remember me saying something about them a couple of days ago. Now those two Grahams was no kin to Tom Graham who got mixed up in the Pleasant Valley War."

"They'd rustled some cattle, as I remember."

"That's right, and I knew where they was squatting, in a dugout that somebody else'd built and abandoned. Happens, you know, people'll set sight on a piece of land and build a cabin or maybe a dugout as part of the improvements. Anyhow, I knew the place, which lay a little south of Cottonwood Wash and this side of Cherry Creek."

"They know you?"

"I reckon. Not many rannies around what hadn't heard of C. P. Owens's shooting, or what I did to thieving Navajos what tried to steal my purebred horses. Yeah. They knew me. And I knew them, to see 'em."

"Were they your first arrests?"

"Not hardly. When I got over to their homestead, they was nobody there. Vacant. Not even a ghost."

"Ran?"

"George, he left a note pinned to the door with a darning needle. It said they was leaving Apache County, and had no intentions of ever coming back. Well, that was OK by me. Not necessary to plug a outlaw if he's willing to leave the county and never return. That was something Andy Cooper could never understand. That Pleasant Valley got his blood heated up to where he figured they weren't nobody with enough gumption to go up against him. He was wrong, and so was anyone else who thought like that."

108

"Sounds like the smart thing to do."

"Smart ain't often a word a person uses when talking about lawbreakers. Lots are just ordinary folks like you and me, but who took a wrong turn somewhere along the line, like I pert near did. Some're stupid as a pine board, but figure they're smarter than any man who wears a badge. They're lucky one time, robbing a stage or some such, and figure every job they'll ever pull will go the same way."

"The James boys seem to have done quite well."

C.P. gave me one of his eyes-only smiles. "You'd think so, but who was it what got shot in the back of the head by someone who was supposed to be his friend?"

"Jesse James."

"And that Northfield Minnesota raid by the Jameses and Youngers. Ask me, that was a long way to ride for nothing more than a belly full of lead. Not smart. Not smart at all."

"But there were some smart ones, outlaws, I mean. Isn't that true?"

"Me? I only met two in all my years of wearing a badge. Only two." C.P.'s eyes took on a faraway look like he was going back over the years to meet those outlaws again.

"I'd like to hear about those two smart outlaws, if I could," I said. "Who were they?"

"Kid Swingle and Red McNeil. That's who they were."

1

Back in those days, lots of youngsters got tagged with "kid." Just off the top of my head I can remember Billy the Kid, Apache Kid, Kid Johns, Kid Blue, Sweetwater Kid, and more recently, Sundance Kid. I wonder if him and Butch really did buy the farm down there in Bolivia.

Swingle's name was Grant, but I don't know if he were named after the general. He showed up in Apache County not long before I got elected sheriff. Said he was cowboying at Ab Johnson's spread over in the Luna Valley area of New Mexico. When I seen him at the Bucket of Blood in Holbrook, he looked like any other rannie, and he seemed a little green, you know, like he wasn't quite able to make sense of things like a growed man would, though he was twenty-three at the time. He was quick to laugh and didn't seem to mind being the butt of all the other cowpokes' jokes.

I saw him a couple of times there in Holbrook and we knew each other enough to nod in passing. Then, not more'n two months after I was sworn in sheriff, Kid Swingle went and robbed the stage that ran from Navajo Springs to St. Johns and on to Fort Apache and San Carlos. The stage hadn't gone more than eight miles or so when the kid stopped it in the bottom of a gully. There weren't no shotgun rider, and no passengers. Just Carl Waite, the mail, and a strong box with army pay in it.

Kid Swingle tied Carl up, broke the strong box open, emptied it, and rode away with pert near ten thousand bucks in double eagles. He never killed no one, but he couldn't keep his hands off other men's things.

Anyway, I got Judge Westover to issue a warrant on the Kid . . . on Grant S. "Kid" Swingle, and I put a general "wanted" wire on the telegraph so's lawmen'd know that anyone, any big spender, might be the Kid.

Now, Kid Swingle weren't no little kid, at least in years, him being born in '63. But he wasn't a big man, that is, not all that tall nor big around. In fact, lots of men could look down at him and maybe beat him at arm wrestling. Not sure but what he didn't start people calling him "kid" because that made him out as nothing to be afraid of. And that big smile on his freckled face. That smile got him more than the business end of any six-gun.

The kid was born in Missouri, at least he said he was. And it may be that with all them double eagles in his saddlebags, that he headed home to live out his days on the family farm, if that's what the family had.

I say that because first thing I know, little Joey

Hendricks comes running in with a yellow paper for me. Yellow paper means telegram most of the time, and this one come addressed to C. P. Owens, Sheriff of Apache County, Territory of Arizona. The sender was Harlan Ellison, Sheriff of Henry County in Missouri. GRANT SWINGLE RE YOUR WARRANT SEEN IN CLINTON STOP ADVISE STOP

I sent a wire back. HOLD PENDING MY ARRIVAL STOP OWENS

I put out the word for Kid Swingle's apprehension, and Harlan Ellison caught sight of him. It's a hell of a long ways from Holbrook, Arizona, to Clinton, Missouri. And I was sitting in the sheriff's office in St. Johns, fifty miles from the nearest train station.

As I'd bring Kid Swingle back to St. Johns in shackles, I saw no need to carry more than my regular .44 Remington.

I rode to my cabin at Cottonwood Seep, bathed and changed clothes, polished my badge, cleaned and loaded the Remington, filled the loops of my gunbelt with cartridges, and rode a gentle bay Morgan that was related to the Morg horse I first brought to Arizona.

I left the bay at Brown's Livery in Holbrook and walked to the station. "I'll be needing a ticket to Clinton, Missouri, and back, William," I said.

William Rogers licked a finger and leafed through his little book of fares. "Lemme see.

113

You can take the A and P from here to Amarillo." He flipped through a few more pages. "Ah, yes. Change trains there and head for Guthrie in the Nations. From there you can ride the West Missouri Railroad to where you're going. Shouldn't be no trouble at all."

"How much you figure it's gonna cost?" I like to keep good records of any money I pay out for the county, and fetching Kid Swingle back from Clinton, Missouri, is surely county business.

"I can give you a round-trip ticket for twenny-five bucks, cash. If I can ask, why in the world're you goin' to Clinton, C.P.?"

"Prisoner. Sheriff in Henry County says he's got an eye on Kid Swingle."

"Then you'll be bringing another passenger on the way back?"

"I reckon you could say that."

"The fare'll be forty bucks for the both of you then."

I paid him with greenbacks and four-bit coins. William gave me a receipt and made out the tickets.

"Train'll pull out at four twenny-four this afternoon," William said.

"Four twenty-four? To the minute?"

"Folks find four twenny-four easy to remember. Don't really matter what time it really leaves. Oh, we keep to a schedule pretty good, but a minute or two don't make that much difference."

"I'll be here." And I was, carrying my six-gun and a pair of manacles for Swingle. A&P called their passenger train "The Flyer," but it rarely went faster than thirty miles an hour. Still, we covered more ground in a couple of hours than you'd want to ride a horse over in a day.

I'll have to admit, I slept most of the way to Amarillo. Hadn't been out from under the pressure of that sheriff's badge for months. And them county supervisors push. Seems they expect a badge to turn a man into some kind of law machine. In fact, the conductor's hand on my shoulder is what woke me.

"Amarillo coming up, Sheriff. You'll want to get over to the eastern-most track. That'll be three platforms over from where we let you off. We're coming in at twelve to noon and your train's scheduled to move out at one. That's gives you an hour—other train's already at the platform, so you can climb aboard any time you like before one."

I thanked the conductor and collected my carpetbag from the rack over the seats. There were a dozen or so travelers in the car, but no faces I could put a name to, and sleeping had precluded making lots of friends on the way to Guthrie. I'm not too much of a talker anyway. Now Jim Houck, he could make friends with a Rocky Mountain spotted skunk and come out smelling like a rose. Me, I just shut up and keep to myself. That's the safest way, I figure.

Amarillo to Guthrie's a jaunt. I didn't feel too good about getting back into the Indian Nations, but I wasn't going into no town, so I just tipped my hat over my eyes and slept . . . or at least looked like I was sleeping.

The train got to Guthrie just before noon, and they were holding the Western Missouri train for me to get on.

Clinton being a railroad town, I was a bit surprised the train from Guthrie wasn't longer— four cars and a caboose. "Been waiting for you, Sheriff," the conductor said. "Climb aboard and we'll get this here train on its way."

"I'm here," I said, and swung aboard. I'd no more than put a foot on the steps up into the car than the conductor was waving his white flag, telling the engineer to pull out.

How Harlan Ellison knew which train I was on, I'll never know, but he was waiting at the platform when I stepped from the second car from the last.

"Sheriff Owens?"

"I am."

"We've got an eye on that boy Swingle, Sheriff."

"Making any trouble?"

"Nah. He seems to be a nice boy. Hasn't robbed anyone hereabouts."

"He'll walk off with your britches, you don't watch close."

"They say he don't look like a bad kid. Don't sound like one either, from what I hear."

"Like I said, his fingers are a mite stickier than most." We walked along the street that ran perpendicular to the railway station. The sheriff never made a move to hail one of the cabs clopping along the way, so I took it that wherever we were going, it weren't too far away. Still, we walked a good thirty minutes, turning two corners as we went.

"Be it ever so humble," Ellison said, sweeping his hand out to indicate a cut-stone building, two stories high, with a sign on the front that said HENRY COUNTY in foot-high letters.

"Yeah." I gave him a little grin. "Humble to y'alls, high falutin' to cowpokes like me."

Ellison led me into the building. "Sheriff Owens from Arizona," he said to the man at the desk.

"He come looking for that kid, Sheriff?"

"I reckon. Be good to have him out of Missouri."

"C. P. Owens," I said, angling my chest so the man could see my sheriff's badge, "Sheriff of Apache County, Arizona."

"Yessir." The man at the desk stood. I thought for a minute he was going to salute.

"Cavalry or infantry?" I said.

The man grinned. "Cavalry. Seventh. Company K under Benteen, sir. Mustered out in '83. Been policing ever since. O'Hara's the name."

"Pleased." I stuck out a hand and O'Hara shook it.

Ellison got us settled in his office, then he hollered for someone name of Griddle.

"You call, Sheriff?"

Griddle stood in the doorway, five-six high and near that wide. Stocky is not a word broad enough for him.

"Any idea where that Kid Swingle is right now?"

"Humansville, I hear."

"What? Humansville?"

"That's what I hear."

Ellison turned his attention to me. "C.P., I would have thought he'd stick around, but it seems the boy has gone to Humansville."

"Where's that?" No use for me to complain. I'd come for Kid Swingle, and it was up to me to catch him.

Thing is, he weren't in Humansville, neither hide nor hair. So I went on to Springfield. The Kid weren't there either, so I ended up back in Clinton. Sheriff Ellison had more news for me. "Your man's in Morgan, Texas."

"Where in God's country is Morgan, Texas?"

"You'll have to take a round-about way by train. Find a way from here to Fort Worth, then you get a Texas and Pacific train toward El Paso, Morgan'll be on that line."

Took me nearly two weeks to make Morgan, it being one of those way-out towns. Like at Clinton, the marshal was at the station when the Texas & Pacific train pulled in. He stood tall in the harsh Texas sunlight, dressed in a black sack suit, buttoned at the top. Couldn't see a badge or gun, but I figured they were there somewhere.

"Sheriff Owens?"

"Your town's a helluva long ways from nowhere. Yes. I'm C. P. Owens."

"Received your telegram, Sheriff. Grant Swingle's in our jail."

"Much obliged, Marshal. Been chasing that boy since he left Arizona."

"We can walk to the jail. It's a bit off the main drag, but not too far."

Indeed the jail at Morgan, Texas, stood apart. The town clustered around the railway station with corrals on the northwest corner, a saloon or two to the east of the corrals, and several businesses south of the tracks. There was even a couple of churches. The jailhouse was of sandstone, a single small cabin-looking affair with one cell.

"Looks like you don't have room for many wrongdoers in Morgan," I said.

"Got our share. Betimes, men sleep off their likker on the floor in there."

"C.P.? Is that you, C.P.?" The voice came from the jail. " 'Bout time you came for me. I been stuck in this rock vault for nigh on ta two weeks."

"We'll start for Holbrook in the morning," I said to Kid Swingle. "You walked away from the stage with a bunch of gold double eagles. Go easier on you if the lion's share of that loot was to get back to the army."

The Kid smiled big and wide, showing all his teeth. His light-blue eyes had a sparkle to them. "Why, C.P., I never heard of no loot. How much is it I oughta have?"

"Ten thou or so in gold coins."

The Kid laughed out loud. "Do I look like a man with that kind of money?"

To be truthful, he didn't. But then, a man don't always look like what he is. I turned to go.

"Hey, C.P."

I stopped, but didn't turn.

"Why not let it go? No one hurt. Government money missing, they say, but don't the government just take away from us'ns anyway? An' what does the army do but hold dances and plays and stuff for officers? Men don't get a living wage and have fatigue duty six days a week or more."

I didn't answer. A little farther on, I turned and said, "Tomorrow morning, Kid. That's when we start for Holbrook."

2

Kid Swingle was bright-eyed and bushy-tailed when the marshal and I got him from the jail. "C.P., I'm awful rank. Smell like a two-year-old skunk. Be nice to have a bath before we go. Don't need a shave."

"Where's the loot, Kid?"

"Don't know what you're talking about, C.P."

"He didn't have but six dollars and fifty-three cents on him," the marshal said. "We went to his room at Brightly's place, but there was nothing in his carpetbag but an extra shirt and a pair of long handles. We got 'em over to the office."

"OK. You get a bath, Kid. I don't want to ride all the way to Arizona upside a skunk." I figured I could get Kid a talking and he'd let slip what he'd done with all that money, but it didn't quite work out that way.

Out in the light of day, Kid Swingle didn't look more'n maybe thirteen years old. I know I say that a lot, but it's true. He had a little fuzz on his cheeks, freckles on his face, red hair in an unruly mop, and that never-ending toothsome smile.

After we got to the office, the marshal gave

121

me directions to a barber what had baths as well, so I herded the Kid down the street in that direction.

Back in Holbrook, a man never seen many women just walkin' the street. Here in Morgan, there was women all over the main part of town, most of them wearing bustles and toting parasols. Ever one of them eyed the manacles on the Kid's wrists and looked at me like I was some kind of brute that beat up on little kids. The Kid thought it was funny.

"Hey, C.P., whyn't you take these here cuffs off me and I'll promise not to run away."

"Kid, I trust you about as far as I can throw an ox by the tail."

He laughed, but there was something in his eyes that made me want to be extra careful.

The barber was finishing up a customer's face with a straight razor. He didn't even look up when we walked in. "With you in a minute, gents," he said. "Just have a seat."

We did, and with Kid Swingle sitting right next to me, I got a good whiff of what he meant when he said him and a two-year-old skunk was closer than cousins.

The barber took a steaming towel to his customer's face, and then dumped some mint water on his hands and slapped it on. "There ya go, Ed," he said, and whipped off the sheet-lookin' affair he'd had covering the man.

"Thank ya, Bart," the man called Ed said. "Always gives a man a boost to get a close shave in the morning." He paid Bart the barber two bits and left with little more than a glance at the Kid and me.

"What'll it be, gents?"

"The Kid says he needs a bath, and after sitting next to him, I have to agree."

"Baths are ten cents cold, two bits hot."

"Hot," the Kid said.

"Hot," I said. I'd pay from the Kid's money, which the marshal had given me when we left his office.

"Out back. Take your hot water from the heater. Soap 'n towel in the cubicle."

"Wow, cubicle," the Kid said. "High falutin'. Let's go." He headed for the back door.

Two cubicles and a hot water heater that ran on coal. Good setup as setups go. The Kid held his arms out at me with a question in his eyes.

"Not a chance," I said.

"Can't get outta my shirt or my long johns with my hands cuffed," he said.

"Oh. Yeah." I unlocked one cuff so the Kid could undress. I drew my Remington and sat on a bench. "Don't try anything," I said. "You wouldn't be the first outlaw I shot for resisting arrest." I thumbed the hammer back and kept my attention on the Kid.

He bathed and came out smelling like a rose.

Well, not exactly like a rose, but flowery. I reckon it was that new-fangled soap he'd used. Even though he dressed in clean long johns and a fresh shirt, the Kid looked dissatisfied.

"What?"

"C.P., I really do need a new pair of pants. Canvas ones'd be good."

"Train's leaving directly."

"A couple of minutes, C.P."

"We'll ask the barber if there's a general store between here and the station. We'll see."

"Socks'd be good, too."

Luckily, there was a store on the way, so we arrived at the Morgan station with the Kid shining like a new penny with both hands in manacles, of course. The train had a head of steam up and chuffed out of the station almost before we got all the way up the steps to the passenger car.

"Bo-o-oard. Bo-o-oard. All the way to Sierra Bianca and beyond. All the way. Bo-o-oard."

There wasn't nobody on the platform, but the conductor hollered anyway. Made no matter that the cars were clacking into motion as the locomotive chugged ahead, laboriously pulling car after car until the whole train moved west on the Texas & Pacific tracks.

The Kid caused no problem. Meek as a lamb. I shoulda known he had something more than his arm up his sleeve.

As we sat facing each other, the Kid, not like usual, didn't have much to say. But a kid like him can't shut up for long. "You know I ain't done nothing wrong, don't you, C.P.?"

"I know that Carl Waite said it was you what held up his mail stage. The judge believed him, too, and that's why I've got a warrant for your arrest. Any time you make off with U.S. government money, they ain't gonna quit until your behind is in Yuma Prison and you've got a few years and some time in the Snake Den to consider the gravity of your crimes."

He pouted and pulled the brim of his floppy hat down over his eyes. I reckon he figured I wasn't gonna be no soft touch, just because he looked so young and innocent. He let out a sigh, like I'd done him wrong, or something, but I didn't take the bait. We stayed that way, him with the floppy hat down over his face, me watching the country rush by the window at about thirty miles an hour.

The Kid looked like he was sleeping, but he kept moving his hands, like the cuffs were bothering him. Then he said, "C.P., these shackles is awful tight. Would you mind loosening them a notch?"

A lawman doesn't always have his good sense alive and well. That was one of those times. I dug out the key and loosened the cuffs one notch each. Didn't notice at the time that the Kid kept both hands doubled up into fists.

"That better?"

"Thank you, C.P. Lots better." The Kid settled back, the floppy hat down over his eyes. He went to sleep. At least that's what I thought.

There are times when a man needs to stand next to a pole and relieve himself. I'm not a drinker, of spirits that is, so the urge don't hit me so often as some, but the urge came some miles east of a little town called Tonah in West Texas. The Kid was asleep and shackled, so I took myself to the washroom to bleed the lizard and slap a little water on my face. I wasn't gone more than five minutes, all told. But when I got back, the Kid's manacles, still locked, were right there on his seat, and he was gone. The window was open. Naturally, I jerked the bell rope, and the train screeched to a halt some miles down the line. We went back and forth, looking, but never found hide nor hair of Kid Swingle. I couldn't figure no way he could get away without help, and said so. Some took that to mean I was passing the buck. That ain't it. I just couldn't think of any other way.

In the end, I figure he climbed onto the undercarriage of a car, maybe even the car we was in, and rode to the end of the line in Sierra Bianca. Then he could've hitched a ride in a boxcar, or something, on to Arizona. I say that because not long after, the Kid was found dangling from a telegraph pole in Clifton, Arizona, which is out of my jurisdiction. Seems he'd taken the wrong man's horse. In the end, his thieving ways caught up with him.

3

Now, I consider myself as smart as most ordinary men, but like I said, I only got about three years of schooling. You know, the kind where you sit at a desk and some schoolmarm drills you in alphabet and handwriting and history and so on. Three years ain't enough to pick up much, so I'm not apt to write a lot. Whenever I put pen to paper, people can tell I've got no schooling. It's just that I never had the chance.

Red McNeil was a smart ass. He liked to make fun of me, and rightfully so, I reckon, him being educated and all. It all started, as far as I was concerned, with Red trying to rob A&B Schuster's general store in Holbrook. It was early June as I recollect. Red went into Schuster's late, about an hour before midnight, when Adolf Schuster—the "A" of A&B—was just getting ready to close the store for the day.

Well, Red McNeil come busting in, a six-shooter in each hand. He shoved one into Adolf's soft middle and told him to open the safe, or get ready to meet St. Peter.

Thing was, Ben Schuster—the "B" of A&B—was in the back room getting ready for bed. He could hear what Red McNeil said, plain as day, so he lit out the back door, looking for help.

"Fellas, there's a gunsharp robbing our store. He's got a gun in Adolf's gizzard. We need to help him," says Ben when he got to the saloon.

Two patrons volunteered and looked for their weapons while Ben got a double-barreled shotgun from the barbershop next door, and three men, armed and dangerous, went in the front door to face down the robber.

"We gotcha!" Ben hollered. "You'd better throw them six-guns down and put your hands up."

Red just laughed. He stuck one pistol into his waistband and grabbed Adolf, whose portly shape was plenty of protection for Red. He sidled toward the back door, and when he got there, he pushed Adolf away and dodged out the door just as Ben touched off one barrel of the 10-gauge he'd borrowed. Most of the pellets chewed into the doorjamb, and Red just kept on going.

Next morning, the Schusters took a good look at the shotgunned doorjamb and saw that there were bits of cloth in some of the pellet holes, so they figured the robber'd been grazed at least.

I've been saying "Red" all this time because that smartass never even tried to cover up his face or throw people off with some kind of disguise. Adolf knew him. "I tried to talk Red outta robbing us, but he just laughed. 'No jail can hold me,' Red said. 'You open up that safe and save yourself getting hurt.'"

Thing was, Red McNeil never hurt no one,

even though he stole stuff right and left, mostly horses.

At the time he tried to rob the Schusters, Red had already escaped jail twice, once in Phoenix and once in Florence. But that was none of my business as it happened outside Apache County. Red was supposed to have rode for the Hashknife Outfit for a while, but I never came across him. So when the court put out a warrant for his arrest, I didn't know him by sight and could only hit up them who did know him. Chances were they'd be able to tell me where he was.

Like I said, Red McNeil was a smartass. He left a poem pinned to a box elder tree just west of Horsehead Crossing on the Little Colorado. I still remember what it said.

> I am king of the outlaws / I am perfection at robbing a store / I have a stake left me by Wells Fargo / And before long, I will have more.
>
> On trains I have made a good haul / Stages are the things that I hate / My losses are always small / My profits exceedingly great.
>
> I will say a few words for my friends / You see I have quite a few / And although we are at dagger's ends / I would like to say, "How'd ya do."
>
> There are McKinney and Larsen, / Who

say that robbers have no honor / I think in a test of manhood / They'd have to stand back in the corner.

They are my kind friends, the Schusters, / For whom I carry so much lead / In the future to kill this young rooster / They will have to aim at his head.

Commodore Owens says he would like to kill me / To me that sounds like fun / 'Tis strange he would thus try to kill me / The red headed son-of-a-gun.

He handles the six shooter mighty neat / And kills a jack-rabbit every pop / But should he and I happen to meet / There'll be a regular old Arkansas hop.

My friends, I have to leave you / My war horse is sniffing the breeze / I wish I could stay here to see you / Make yourselves at home, if you please.

I will not say very much more, / My space is growing small / You're always welcome to my share / What's that? "Much obliged." Not at all.

Yours in luck,
R.W. McNeil

Damn his eyes.

People laughed behind my back. I know they did. All because of Red McNeil. That made it all the more important that I catch him.

I'd been over to Heber and rode northeast toward Holbrook. I'd gotten out of the pine trees that line the rim country and was crossing Hashknife range when I come across a young cowboy.

"Evening," says I.

"Sheriff Owens," he said. "I see you are a long way from St. Johns."

"Don't spend much time there," says I. "Too many owlhoots out and around."

"You don't say?" He sounded like an educated man by the way he spoke. "Who might you be expecting to arrest in this area?"

"Arrest? No one, lest I run across that robber Red McNeil. You seen him lately?"

"Who did you say?"

"Red McNeil. Know him?"

The cowboy grinned. "Can't say that I do."

"Someone around'll know him," I said.

"Say. I'm headed for the Hashknife line camp on Sherlon's Fork. Those men may know something about . . . Who was it you were looking for?"

"Red McNeil."

"Oh yes. Red McNeil. What do you say?"

"Might as well. Lead on."

There were six men, a dutch oven full of beef and beans and a pot of coffee at the line camp. Naturally they asked us to light and set.

"I'm looking for a robber named Red McNeil,"

I said after having a bait of beans and a cup of coffee. "Heard he rode for the Hashknife. Any a you men seen him lately?"

They looked kinda surprised and looked back and forth from me to the cowboy I'd rode in with.

"Red McNeil? Don't recollect seeing much of him lately," one of the Hashknifers said. The other men kinda mumbled and murmured the same thing.

"Well, if it's all right with you cowboys, I'll spend the night here and get off to Holbrook in the morning."

"Fine, Sheriff. Pick any soft spot you see around that's not already got soogans on it."

I got my bedroll from behind my saddle, took the tack off my horse and picketed him, and rolled my soogans out.

"Looks like you've got quite a big ground cloth," the young cowboy said. "All I got is one measly blanket and a worn out slicker. Would you mind if I shared your ground cloth for the night?"

I'm not one to be chintzy with them what's worse off than me, so I said, "You're welcome. And you can use my saddle blanket to cover you if you should get cold."

"I'll do that, Sheriff. Are you sure you're in the right business?"

"Being sheriff? That's what I was elected to do, son. I'll give 'er my best shot."

While me and the cowboy were talking, the Hashknife bunch was sitting awful still around the fire, staring into their coffee cups when they weren't sipping from them. Once in a while one would shake his head, as if he couldn't believe what was going on. I spread my tarp full out and laid my soogans on one half. The young cowboy could have the other half. We retired at the same time, but the cowboy was asleep long before I dropped off.

I woke at dawn as usual, but the young cowboy had risen and rode away without waking me, to which I paid little mind. The Hashknife men invited me to breakfast of bacon and saleratus biscuits, which I gladly accepted.

"So you're after Red McNeil, are you?" said a Hashknife rannie.

"I am. He's a robber who ain't afraid of nothing. He never even covered his face when he tried to rob Adolf Schuster."

"Didn't they tell you what he looks like?"

"In a way. They said he's a little above average height, but not as tall as me. An' they figured he had blue eyes, but wasn't sure, it being almost midnight when he held up Adolf and Ben Schuster's general store."

"Hmmm," the Hashknife boys said, and went to sipping at their strong black coffee.

"McNeil worked for the Hashknife Outfit. Do any of you boys know him? Could any of you tell me more about him so's I'll know him if ever I run across him?"

"That's almighty strange, Sheriff. We'd a thought you'd know Red McNeil up close and personal, being as you rode in with him last night."

You could have knocked me over with a broom straw.

The Hashknife boys laughed like it were a good joke on me. And I reckon it was.

"Dang"—I don't like to cuss—"Dang. Whyn't none of you rannies tell me I was riding with Red McNeil?"

"Didn't want no blood dirtying up our camp. If'n we'd a said something like 'Hiya Red,' then there'd a been shootin', sure as Christmas. We didn't want no one shot."

I had no answer to that, because if Red McNeil had drawed iron on me, he'd a sure been a dead man.

"Red left this for you." The head cowboy held out a piece of paper. I took it. Red McNeil'd writ in near-perfect hand:

Pardon me, Sheriff
I'm in a hurry;
You'll never catch me,
But don't you worry.
                    —Red McNeil

I never did catch Red. He'd made a fool outta me, but then, it weren't the first time. Still, his making fun of me started people thinking that I couldn't run the sheriff's office quite right and that I wouldn't be the proper man to maintain law and order in Apache County.

Part V

The Snider Gang

I could tell Commodore Owens had not been comfortable during yesterday's session. It seemed he felt that his first term in office had served more to damage his image than to build it up.

He seemed straightforward and honest, but I have no idea how well he did as a leader of men. From the record, it seems he did much better when acting on his own, taking blame or credit on his own, and not having to answer to what others—deputies and such—did in his stead.

This morning I had reached the Bucket of Blood before Commodore Owens arrived. Only Frick the barman was there.

"C.P. around?"

"Ain't here yet," Frick said. "Should be afore long, though. Coffee?"

"Coffee'd be good." I'd had two cups, maybe three, while ingesting the good breakfast food at the Havasu House. Fred Harvey sure knew how to set a table, and how to pick those who served. Don't know a man alive who would bitch about being served by a Harvey Girl.

137

Frick had no more than brought me the cup of coffee he promised than Commodore Owens slid in the front doors. He said nothing. Frick the barman said nothing. I said nothing.

He sat opposite me.

Frick brought him a cup of coffee, setting it in front of him almost before he got completely situated in his chair. He still said nothing, and he didn't really look me in the eye. It was like he didn't register my presence.

He drank all the coffee. I drank all my coffee. Frick brought more coffee. Nobody said a thing.

Finally, C.P. looked at me. "How's your morning, shaver?"

"Can't complain, C.P. We have to take what comes, but at the Havasu House, what comes is better than most."

"I hear you're sweet on Betty McNeil."

I had to raise my eyebrows. She was sweet, but taking good care of me, a Havasu House guest, was part of her job. And I didn't mean anything disrespectful when I say that. "She's a Harvey Girl. They're paid to look after Fred Harvey's guests."

"You don't say. Well, you be real careful or you'll have both barrels of Randolf McNeil's 12-gauge up your rear end as you head for the J.P."

"Speaking of girls, C.P., we've never talked about all your girlfriends."

"Nothing to say."

"I hear that you were sweet on a Mexican girl in St. Johns."

"It don't matter. Over and gone. 'Sides, no woman ever got in the way of what had to be done."

"What had to be done?"

"My job was to get rid of the outlaws in Apache County. That's what I figured anyway. The supervisors thought otherwise, though. They wanted me out there running my horses all over the county collecting fees and fines and whatever they could come up with to put money in the coffers. But I was out after outlaws . . . and not all of them were out on the range."

Commodore Perry Owens, never famous for his smile, kept a straight stone-hard face. Thinking back on his Apache County sheriff days never brought humor to his face.

"Being sheriff is not such a posh post, I guess," I said.

"Like I said, I was elected to rid the county of outlaws. They what stole critters was easy enough to run down, but as soon as the crime took place in someone's fine paneled office, every man and his dog looked for ways to trip me up."

"Sounds like you might be talking about John Blevins."

"Him, and Tony Perez, and Sol Barth, and a bunch more from the St. Johns Ring."

"But didn't John Blevins become a lawman later on?"

"He did. That don't change the fact that he was ruled guilty by a jury and then pardoned by the governor, who didn't know up from down about what John Blevins did or did not do."

"But wasn't that kind of the way things often went? In looking through the records of inmates at Yuma Territorial Prison, before it was moved to Florence, I remember seeing many inmates pardoned by governors."

"That don't make it right every time. Fact is, I'd be willing to bet that most who were in Yuma deserved to be there."

"Be that as it may, can we get back to talking about how you cleaned outlaws out of Apache County?"

"Lots of 'em skedaddled when I got elected."

"But not all?"

Commodore shook his head. "Not by a long shot." He held his coffee mug up and Frick rushed to get it refilled.

"Which ones come to mind?"

"You mean besides the Blevins family?"

I nodded. "If you please."

Commodore stared at the tabletop for a long moment, his face set in flat, hard lines, as if remembering was not a pleasant task. "You know," he said, "most folks never knew what I did to rid this country of owlhoots. I guess nobody paid much attention. Not that I was hunting glory or anything like that, but all the news rags would say was, 'Sheriff Owens left town on official business and returned empty-handed.' Of course I never told any reporter—other than yourself—what took place in those days when I was out of town on 'official business.'"

"And what might that business have been?"

"You asked me that before, and I'm getting around to it." Commodore's blue eyes took on an icy glint, and his face remained without expression. I got a hint of what it must have been like for a lawbreaker to see the sheriff close up.

"Apologies, C.P. Don't let me interrupt, but which . . ."

"I'm getting to that."

I held my tongue and sat with my Sheaffer poised over the foolscap I used to record Commodore's story in shorthand.

"I reckon it were the gang at Round Valley," Commodore said.

"The Snider Gang?"

"Shut up and let me talk." Commodore stood and walked to the bar, coffee mug in hand. Frick fetched the pot and filled the mug. I had to wonder why Commodore had done that, but I imagine it was because of my incessant questions. I knew I had to give him more breathing space, or run the risk of losing this precious opportunity to record the legendary lawman's own version of his days behind a badge.

The old sheriff sat in silence, sipping at his coffee. He gazed at the front window, but his eyes seemed not to focus. Perhaps they were seeing events of long ago once again.

"They called it the Snider Gang," Commodore said, "but a fast gun by the name of Ken Grizwold was the mainstay.

"I say fast gun because Griz was always ready to jerk iron and when he did, he pulled the trigger. And I'll tell you again, it ain't how quick you can whip out a six-gun or lever a rifle, it's all about whether you've got the guts and gumption to take the shot and put a man down. Griz was always ready, and I reckon I could count up a dozen men, at least a dozen, he took down with his S 'n' W Russian or the Winchester saddle gun he always carried."

"Snider Gang? An organization? How did it work, may I ask?"

"You know about the Outlaw Trail?"

"I've heard of Hole in the Wall and Robber's Roost, if that's what you mean." Of course, I knew of the Outlaw Trail, and I knew that cattle and horses were moved from and to Canada and Mexico and many places in between. Stolen stock went north and south with everyone sharing in the driving and the profits. I knew, but I wanted to find out why Commodore Owens brought it up.

"Snider's gang cowboyed cattle down the Trail toward Mexico and up the Trail toward Mexican Hat, but Griz worked on the side with a bunch of rannies, robbing a mail stage once in a while, or making off with cows to sell to the Indian Agent in San Carlos. Gus Snider didn't do that, but Ken Grizwold did. Oh, how he did. So when I got elected county sheriff, I got warrants for Grizwold and a dozen of his compadres. Then I went to give them fair warning."

1

Some people think of Arizona as hot and dry. Well, dry she is, but up on the Colorado Plateau and into the foothills of the White Mountains, snow lay a foot deep on the flats and in drifts up to the height of a tall man. True, the country's dry and snow don't fall every day, but in January, it don't melt much either. A man wants to ride careful because the snow's crusted and can cut a horse's fetlocks if you have to ride off the trail for some reason. Still, I was the elected sheriff of Apache County, and I'd promised to rid the county of outlaws.

Some of them took off right away, not wanting to trade shots with me. The owlhoots in Round Valley, though, stayed put. So I went calling.

The Little Colorado runs through Round Valley on its way to St. Johns, the Zuni fork, and north and west to join with the Colorado in the depths of the Grand Canyon. In other words, all I had to do was follow the river uphill.

Just my luck that there's no regular road between St. Johns and Round Valley, but at least I had a choice. I could head southeast toward Escudilla and double back on the mail road, or I could move west through Concho, over the divide, and back southeast to Becker's store.

Julius built his general store at the crossroads where people coming or going to Round Valley, Eager, Springville, or Show Low passed. Julius Becker was no fool. He always did what was good for business.

Julius'd cleared the snow from in front of the store so horses could stand on hard ground. Smoke drifted from the chimney up and across the cloudless sky. I could almost hear the crackle as juniper logs gradually crumbled into coals and then ashes. Had to be warm inside that store, and half a day's ride out of St. Johns, I could use some warming up.

I left Cloudy, my grulla, tied to the rail. He looked at me like he wanted a bait of grain. "Hold on, pard," I said. "Oats as soon as I can get some."

"Gone to talking with your hosses now, have ya?"

I glanced in Julius's direction. "This here horse carries on a better conversation than most men I know." Cloudy give me a nudge with his nose. "An' right now, he'd like some oats. Got any?"

"I do," Julius said, giving me one of his famous smiles, the ones that showed lots of teeth so you'd ignore the eyes. "You being county sheriff makes me wonder why you've come in this direction. Must be cold out on the trail."

"Oats for the horse. And I'm here to have words with the Snider outfit."

146

"I'll get the oats, but words? I've always heard of Commodore Owens talking with his guns. Aren't you the rannie the Navajos call Iron Man?"

"Navajos never could shoot straight. Mind if I come in outta the cold?"

"Open for business, I am."

"Oats for the horse. Can of peaches for me."

"Lemme get 'em. Opened?"

I nodded. "Got me a sweet tooth that wants peaches right this minute."

The goods in Julius Becker's general store stood on the shelves in perfect order. And I didn't see a speck of dust on any of his stock. "You see any of Snider's boys around here much?"

"Couldn't say, Commodore. I don't ask names unless the customer wants credit."

"You know 'em. They around?"

"Winter time don't make for easy pickings. Hard to stay warm." Julius handed me an open can of peaches in syrup and waved me toward a long table surrounded by highback chairs. "You can sit and eat while I get oats for your pony. Mind if I take the bit outta his mouth?"

" 'Bliged," I said, and took him up on the offer. I picked a place not far from the cast-iron stove that sent smoke into the sky through a long black stovepipe and started to work on the can of peaches.

"You got word for Snider's men, you might

want to let me have the message. I'll make sure it gets delivered," Julius said.

"Better to deliver it personal."

"They keep a good watch."

I stabbed the last hunk of peach with my Bowie and ate it. The syrup on those peaches was downright pleasant to drink, and I did.

"I'd better have a box of .44-40s."

"A dime for the peaches, two bits for the oats, half dollar for the bullets," Julius intoned.

"Don't reckon you'd put them on a tab for the county, would ya?"

Julius didn't even crack a smile at my joke. "Cash," he said. "You can collect it from the county later." He plopped the box of fifty rounds on the table. "That'll be eighty-five cents, hard cash."

I paid with paper money.

"Commodore, you be right careful riding into Gus Snider's den," Julius said. "Right careful."

"I'll keep my eyes peeled. Thanks for the peaches, and I hope I don't have to use the ca'tridges."

Julius followed me outside. "You sure I can't deliver your message?" He took the nosebag off Cloudy and bridled him.

I took my Remington .44 from its holster and checked it, spun the cylinder, eared back the hammer, let it down to half cock, added a bullet to the cylinder, and returned the gun to its holster.

Then I pulled the .44-40 Winchester saddlegun from its scabbard, checked the action, levered a round into the chamber, and mounted.

Cloudy gave me an evil eye. "Maybe you want more grain, old boy, but we've got things to do. Giddap."

Cloudy seemed reluctant when I reined him toward the trail to Round Valley. I rode with the Winchester across the saddle bows and the retaining loop off the hammer of my Remington. Cloudy made his way along the one-horse trail as if he knew exactly where he was going. For me, this was the first time I'd started out to visit Gus Snider in his own lair. The saloon came first. No name but SALOON across an old board. If there was any place I could get information, the saloon would be it.

Two horses stood at the rail, a shaggy brown and a three-color paint. I didn't recognize either one, but I hadn't spent any time in Round Valley till now.

I got off Cloudy and left him ground-tied. Winchester in hand, I pushed my way into the saloon.

Not much, as saloons go, a bar running down the north wall, four tables and a back door. Two men, who I figured rode in on the two horses outside, sat at one table, trading poker faces with a ratty gambler. They didn't so much as look up from their cards when I walked in.

Jim McCarthy stood behind the bar. I knew him from Albuquerque. " 'Lo, Jim," I said.

McCarthy kinda grunted. Didn't look too happy to see me. "You'd better look to your hole card, C.P.," he said, "this here's Gus Snider's domain"—McCarthy always used four-bit words—"and he's not partial to lawdogs."

I didn't say nothing, and walked over to stand right in front of him.

"You was elected sheriff of Apache County, I hear," he said.

I just nodded.

"Whatcha want?"

"I come to have a word with Gus Snider and maybe Ken Grizwold." I leaned the Winchester against the front of the bar and put a boot up on the brass foot rail. "Where ought a man go to see Gus Snider?"

"Over to the big house, I reckon."

"Didn't see nothing but tarpapered shacks on the way in."

"The big house is over west of here, behind that little ridge. There's a wagon track you can follow, if you've got the guts."

I gave Jim McCarthy one of my patented lawman smiles. "Now, Jim. You know I've got all the luck I need. Navajos've been bouncing bullets off me for five, six years. That's why they call me Iron Man. Gus Snider's gunhawks ain't got what it takes to down C. P. Owens."

"You talk awful big for one man, C.P."

"Well, being as I'm not a drinking man, I reckon I'll just have to ride on over to Gus Snider's big house and tell him direct." I put four bits on the bar and picked up my rifle. "Thanks for the time."

McCarthy fumed, but he didn't push the coins back across to my side of the bar. The men at the card table ignored me and McCarthy. I touched my forefinger to the brim of my four-by-four hat and left.

Outside, the two horses were still tied to the hitching rail, and Cloudy stood where I'd ground-hitched him. I stood on the saloon's porch for a while to see if anyone left it, front way or back. No one did. Which meant Gus Snider would get no advance warning, or mighty little of it. I shoved the Winchester into the saddle scabbard, mounted, and rode west on a little wagon track, not much more than a couple of ruts in the snow.

2

The rannie on watch stepped out from behind a juniper. I kept both hands on the saddle horn. He didn't point his rifle at me, but it wasn't far off.

"Whatcha think you're doing, C.P.?"

"Ron Lacey. You don't want to go up against me, do you?"

"How'd you know my name?"

"More people know you than you might figure, Ron."

He straightened up and took a stronger grip on his rifle. "Whatcha doing here?"

"Come to have a word with Gus Snider."

"I need to take your hardware," Lacey said.

I shook my head. "No, Ron. I give you my word I'll not use my guns against Gus Snider, but I'll not go naked to see him."

Lacey stood there a while, like thinking and making up his mind was something he didn't do all that often. He gave himself a little nod. "OK, C.P. You just follow me." He started off on the wagon track.

We made our way around that ridge to where we could see the big house, a two-story affair, built like the house of some plantation owner down south.

"Sheriff wants to see Gus," Lacey hollered.

I could see a man in the barn's hayloft off to the south and no doubt there was a long shooter on the ridge. I paid them no special attention.

"Sheriff Owens to see Gus," Lacey hollered again.

A man laid his rifle over the top rail of the ketch pen next to the barn. Another came out the front door, a Greener 12-gauge in the crook of his left arm.

I pulled Cloudy up a few paces away.

"You wanting to see Gus?" the shotgun man asked.

"That's what he said to me," Ron Lacey said.

"That's what I came for," I said.

"You still got your guns." The shotgun inched its way around so it was pointed nearly straight at me.

"I do. I'll not go naked in a rattlesnake den."

"You calling Gus Snider a snake?"

I shook my head. The front door opened. "Let the sheriff in," said a mild voice from inside.

The shotgunner stepped away. I got off Cloudy and left him ground-hitched, knowing he'd be here when I came out. Three steps up to the porch and three strides put me into Gus Snider's big house.

Gus Snider mighta been an outlaw king, but he was a man who liked his comforts, too.

"You might want to lean the long gun against the wall right there," Snider said. His well-modulated voice could have belonged to a slicker. He wore a smoking jacket with a velvet collar, gray flannel trousers, and a pair of carpet slippers. "We can sit to talk. Would you prefer the table or the sofa and armchairs?"

The rich walnut table showed a well-buffed and waxed surface, and ladder-back chairs lined the long sides. One wooden chair with armrests stood at the far end.

"Table looks good," I said.

Snider waved at a chair. "Might want to hang that good Remington on the back. I'll guarantee no one's gonna come in here shooting at you."

"All right." I unbuckled my gunbelt and hung it on the chair Snider pointed at. I sat in the one nearest the end of the table, back to the wall. The grips of my Remington hung less than an arm's length away.

"You're a careful man, Commodore Owens."

"I stay alive, Snider."

"Gus. Call me Gus. There's no need to be all formal." Snider sat in the chair with the armrests.

"Gus."

"Now. You come wearing your brand new sheriff's badge, what can I do for you? Oh. Wait." Snider raised his voice. "Honey, I wonder if you could bring some of your good coffee out for Sheriff Owens? And me, too, if you please." He turned back toward me. "A moment, please, Sheriff—"

"C.P. Most folks call me C.P.," I said.

"Right. C.P."

A young woman came through the door to what I assumed was the kitchen. She carried a fine wooden tray with porcelain cups and saucers, a little pitcher of cream, a sugar bowl, and a small pot of coffee. She poured our coffee, but all her smiles were for Gus Snider.

"My wife, Ellen," he said.

She curtsied. "Pleased," she said.

"Thank you, honey."

"Of course." She disappeared back into the kitchen. I didn't have a chance to say a word to her.

Snider poured a dollop of cream into his cup and dumped in a spoonful of sugar. He stirred the coffee, lifted the cup, and saluted me. "Welcome, C.P. Can't say we're rich, but the good things in life only come once." He sipped the coffee. Rapture showed on his face. "That girl surely brews fine coffee."

I drank mine black, but it was as good as Gus Snider claimed.

"Now. What can I do for you, C.P.?"

"I'm the sheriff now, Gus. And people elected me to put a stop to outlawry here in Apache County."

Snider's eyebrows rose in surprise. "Are you calling me an outlaw, C.P.?"

"If the shoe fits . . ."

Snider gave me a genuine smile. "C.P., I run a bunch of drovers, men good at getting cows and horses from one place to another. Some outfit gets in touch with me, tells me where to pick up the herd and where to deliver it. Then my drovers get paid about a dollar a day, like any other cowboy."

"I know what you do, Gus. Don't know who hires you, and that could make a difference. But I hear that some of them you call drovers are a little hard on the mail stages to Fort Apache, and are not adverse to driving a few head off the range and over the rim to San Carlos. I won't have that, Gus."

Snider didn't look me in the eye, and he took his time with the coffee his wife brought. "I'll be square with you, C.P. I don't own those drovers. And I don't always use the same ones. That means I can't control what they do when they're not working for me."

"Uh huh. So Ken Grizwold gets a free rein, then?"

"He's a good foreman on drives."

"He's a purty good stage robber, too."

Snider made no retort, and his coffee cup was empty.

"You tell him, if you would, Gus, that C. P. Owens says he's to lay off the mail stage and Apache County stock. He doesn't, and I'll come after him with these warrants." I took the warrants from the inside pocket of my vest and laid them on that shiny table. "If you don't want to tell him, Gus, call him in, and I'll tell him myself."

"He could be trouble."

"I've seen trouble before. What'll it be?"

Snider scrubbed the back of his hand across his mouth. He picked up the coffee cup, but it was empty. "Well," he said. "It'll be best if I tell him, I reckon. I'll tell him what you said, and I'll tell you this. If he breaks the law by robbing or rustling, you're free to take him in, if you can get him to go."

"Good enough," I said, and took the last mouthful of that good coffee. "I'll get out of your hair."

I rode Cloudy away from Gus Snider's place, and the lookouts let me go. I hoped he'd make Griz listen. I didn't want to kill nobody.

3

April brings longer days in the high country and the snow cover melted off, mostly. Still froze at night, but daytime could be right pleasant. The county supervisors kept me right busy collecting fees and fines, and I heard nothing of Ken Grizwold until after Easter. The news I got wasn't good.

For a change, I was sitting at my desk in the sheriff's office, glaring at a pile of paperwork. A man would never know that a county sheriff is usually buried under a pile of paper, and people wonder, out loud or in the newspapers, how he can be so slothful and not be out arresting wrongdoers. Now there's a word for you. Wrongdoer.

Jimmy McDougal, the kid that worked cleaning up the place over to the post office, like to busted down the front door. "Sheriff. They done done it again, they did."

"Whoa back, boy. Who done what?"

"They done robbed the mail stage to Fort Apache, done did it and shot Carl Waite, too."

"How's Carl?"

"Dunno. They're bringing him in."

"Who done it?"

"Dunno, but it's done done."

"Who come in with the news?"

"Raymond Westly."

"Where's he?"

"At the Monarch, I reckon."

That made sense. Most men head for a saloon after a long dry ride. I buckled on my Remington and went to the Monarch. Ray Westly was still at the bar.

"Hey, Ray."

" 'Lo, C.P. When you gonna ketch them basties what put lead into Carl Waite and took off with gummit cash?"

"Now, Ray, you know I'll be off after the outlaws as soon as I find out who they are."

"I kin tell ya that."

"Who was it?"

"Who'dja think? Griz and a bunch of Round Valley riders. A whole bunch of them and only one of Carl. He never had a chance."

"Wonder why they shot him?"

"I reckon they wanted him dead. He played that way after them no-gooders plugged him. The team took off when Carl fell out, and the owlhoots went after it. Carl, he just played dead where he fell."

A man come bustin' through the batwings. "Buckboard with Carl Waite just come in," he hollered. "Tooken him over to Doc Miller's place."

None of the drinkers in the Monarch reacted

except me. "Thanks, Ray. I'll get over to the doc's and talk to Carl, if he can talk."

"It were Griz and some Round Valley boys, C.P., just like I said."

"Thanks," I said again, and left.

Raymond Westly was right. At least Carl Waite told me the same story. He never saw whoever shot him, but when he lay on the ground playing dead, he recognized the horses and the one rider who wore a red neckerchief like Ken Grizwold always did.

"They was too far away for me to see faces, C.P., but I could tell Griz from the way he set that roan Appaloosa of his. No question in my mind. Griz and his boys put lead into me and made off with army money and whatever was in the mail sack."

"You rest easy, Carl. I'll get them what done this, and I'll get the money back, too, if I can."

Ken Grizwold had broke the deal I made with Gus Snider. Now it was up to me to make good on my promise. It took me the rest of the day to get ready 'cause I had to get that paperwork done, so I rode out of St. Johns in the late afternoon, begged a place to sleep on the floor of Julius Becker's warm store while Cloudy ate his fill of good oats. Me and Cloudy left as soon as it was light enough to see. That put me on the wagon track to Gus Snider's big house just about breakfast time, me with a loaded Winchester and two pistols—the Remington in its holster and a Colt's Frontier .44-40 behind my gunbelt in the small of my back. That gave me twelve rounds in the pistols and fifteen in the Winchester. I was ready for a small war.

A little over a mile from the big house, I pulled the Winchester, thumbed its hammer back, and jabbed Cloudy with my blunt spurs, which to him was the signal to run. He did.

Ron Lacey, who stopped me before, stepped from behind his cover. My bullet took him high in the center of his chest. He staggered and fell over backward. As Cloudy streaked by, I saw his eyes, open to the sky and sightless. Count one down.

As white men are wont to do, the men at Gus Snider's place shot at me, not Cloudy. Apaches, now, would put me on the ground by shooting my horse. Powder smoke came from the door to the hayloft where I'd seen a rifleman before. I put three shots into the doorway as quick as I could work the Winchester's lever. A man rose, hands clutching his throat, and toppled from the second floor opening. Count two.

But where was the long shooter?

Cloudy thundered by the big house. A bullet took a hunk out of my hat, and another went by my nose, making a slapping sound as it passed. From the layer of gun smoke that hung over the cold ground, a man'da thought we were fighting

Chancellorsville all over again. But no shots came from atop the ridge behind the house. Maybe the long shooter'd not taken his position yet. As Cloudy turned the corner to go between the big house and the horse corral in back of it, I piled off and he kept on running. We'd practiced that move enough that he knew to get away and wait for my whistle.

No sounds of gunfire now. Just the rank smell of burnt gunpowder in the air. I took the lull as a good time to shove half a dozen cartridges into my Winchester's magazine. Half a dozen. I only remembered shooting four times, but a man can't always remember every time he pulls a trigger.

"The star-packer's back of the big house."

"Littleton's gone. Damn sheriff shot 'im right in the eye."

"Shut up and move careful. He's just one shooter."

"Griz. You ain't never had to face Commodore Owens!"

"Ha. I can face any lawdog."

My turn to holler. "That you, Grizwold?"

"I'm right here, and here's where I'll stay."

I scrambled under the lowest pole of the corral and got hid behind one of the big upright posts. The horses gathered on the far side, ears pricked in my direction. I caught the sound of someone scrambling up the side of the ridge. The long shooter?

There. Down low at the north corner of the big house. Someone sticking a head out where the ordinary man would look for one. I lined the Winchester on that head of hair. When the eye came in sight, I put a .44 caliber bullet through it. A blast of red filled with little shards of pink misted out from the corner of the house. The head of hair went motionless. Count three.

The long shooter.

I put my back against the corral post and sat with legs spraddled and knees raised. That way, I could put my elbows on the knees for a solid rest while aiming the Winchester. And that gun sent lead where I pointed it. They didn't name it one-in-a-thousand for nothing. I squinted at the ridge.

Ah. The long shooter carried his weapon in a buckskin boot that covered the whole rifle. Didn't matter if he had a Ballard or a Whitney or a Browning, he was in my sights.

I touched off a .44-40 round.

The bullet thumped into the long shooter just under the ribs of his right-hand side. The angle was such that those 200 grains of lead went busting through his stomach, took out the front half of his heart, then went out just under his left-hand collarbone. He stopped crawling. His leg stretched out, gave a little spasm, and went limp. Count four.

Bullets chewed at the post, but were deflected enough to miss me. A rannie pounded across the open space between the barn and the corral. I let him get to the gap in the corral fence that would give me a good shot at him, then put a bullet into his hipbone, right where the leg connects. He went down with a scream and then started calling for his ma. Count five.

"You ain't gonna get me, Griz," I hollered. "You might as well give up. A few years in Yuma might do you good."

Griz swore a blue streak.

"Cussing ain't gonna do you no good, Griz, and like you can see, Gus is letting you skin your own skunks."

"By the Almighty, Owens, they's four of us and only one of you. You ain't gonna come out alive."

I didn't answer him. I just wiggled myself to the gate, which had double posts at the hinge end to bear the weight of the gate. Behind those thick posts, I stood up. I could hear the sounds of men scrambling for position. I leaned the Winchester against the corral poles and opened the gate enough to slip through. With a Remington in one hand and a Colt's in the other, I strode through the gate and started for the bunkhouse.

Some people'd say I was crazy to walk right out in the open like that, but men hiding get flustered when the other guy takes no notice of them or the hot lead they fling his way.

I took the man at the southeast corner of the big house with a shot from the Colt's. With all the practice I do, shooting at moving tin cans and such, the lead from my handguns goes pretty much where I intend. The bullet from the Colt's went in the back of his hand, smashed his wrist, I reckon, and ranged up through the flesh of his underarm, mangling as it went. Out of action. Count six.

"Come on out, you snakes," I hollered. "Here I am. Right out in plain sight. You all got the gumption to face me and fight?"

A head showed at the west end of the water trough. I put a bullet in it.

Count seven.

Two more. One of them Ken Grizwold.

I stopped almost dead center between the bunkhouse and the big house. I let my six-guns hang in my hands along the seams of my trousers. "You comin' out, Griz? Or are you only good enough to backshoot the driver of a mail stage?"

"I'm here, killer sheriff," Griz shouted, and stood up from where he'd taken cover behind the woodpile.

"How do you want to do it, Griz? Face to face at thirty feet? Step it off like the Louisiana boys do? Free for all, you two against me? Your call."

Griz stalked around the woodpile. "You lousy son," he hollered. "I'll take you here and now." He raised his cocked pistol, but before he could pull the trigger, a bullet from the Remington in my right hand smashed him in the chest, just to the left of his brisket. His mouth opened and closed like a carp out of water. He went to his knees, then fell on his face.

I put my six-shooters away. "Son," I called. "Griz might have seemed like a big strong man to you, but you can see right now that robbing and rustling and such don't pay. Now you're a youngster so I'll look the other way while you skedaddle. You hear me?"

"Yessir," the youngster said.

"I'm going inside to talk to Gus Snider. You be gone when I come out and I'll never say you were here with Ken Grizwold. You hear?"

"Yessir."

Folks say I killed nine of the Snider Gang that April morning, but I only killed six and wounded two.

Epilogue

Arizona's Fondly Remembered Lawman

Most people with any interest in the history of Arizona know that Commodore Perry Owens's single term as Apache Country Sheriff was not his last as a lawman. W. R. Campbell won the election of 1892 and the moment he took the oath in 1893, he hired C. P. Owens as chief deputy. Most everyone who knew him held that he was a topnotch peacekeeper.

That job didn't last long, though, because William Kidder Meade, U.S. Marshal of Arizona Territory, appointed him Deputy U.S. Marshal for the district of Arizona just six months later.

C.P. and I were in our fifth day of conversing at the Bucket of Blood in Seligman, and I wanted to learn what had happened to Owens during his later years of enforcing the law.

Frick had coffee in a mug and on the table by the time I sat down at our regular place. I was on my second cup by the time C.P. walked in. For some reason, his step didn't seem as sure and powerful as before. He blinked and swiped at his eyes with the back of his hand. I couldn't believe it. Commodore Perry Owens, the lawman with the level steely-eyed stare, had blinked. Something didn't seem right.

"Frick," I said. "C.P. doesn't appear well. Does this kind of thing happen often?"

The barman took a moment to answer. He looked at C.P., but the old lawman's eyes were unfocused and his steps faltering. C.P. put a hand on the bar for support. He bowed his head as if in prayer.

"C.P.'s not been all right since him and Miz Lizzie come back from visiting folks in Indiana. Most days he's good, but sometimes he's like now."

He came out from behind the bar and took C.P. by the arm. "Ye're looking spry this morning, C.P. Come on over to yer table. Mr. Evanston's a waiting."

"Evanson? Who's that?"

"Man from Phoenix."

"Where?"

C.P. followed where Frick led him, but didn't seem to know who the bartender was. Frick turned him around and sat him in the chair opposite me. "Here's Mr. Evanston," he said, waving his hand at me. "Hang on a minute, C.P., I'll be getting you a cup a jamoka."

C.P. stared at me. "Tell me, Kid," he finally said. "How'd ya get outta them handcuffs down to Tonah? Tell me that and I'll letcha go."

"C.P., my name is Alexander Evanston. I'm a reporter for the Phoenix Sun."

He grinned. "I remember when you went by Claude Preston, Kid. Did you think that'd fool anyone? Huh? A man can change his name, but there ain't no way he can change his face. After riding all the way from Morgan with you on that forsaken train, you figure I'd forget?"

So I played the part of Kid Swingle in C.P.'s dream world. I don't know what happened to him to throw him off like that, but I never got to talk to him again about his lawman days. I left for Phoenix the next day.

I never got to meet Elizabeth Barrett Owens, but I have heard and read that she was a solid, no-nonsense woman. In the failing months of his life, the woman everyone knew as Lizzie cared for C.P. hand and foot, even though he no longer knew who she was. In those final days, C.P. thought the Blevins boys had come back from the grave to "get" him. Perhaps they did. Perhaps those ghosts stole his mind. Perhaps they just let his body live on and on.

Commodore Perry Owens died in bed on May 28, 1919. He was 67 years old.

As I said, I never again was privileged to talk to him about the old days, so I must summarize his story from my research.

Actually, there's one more tidbit I should add first. During a lull in the conversation on the third day, I found the courage to ask C.P. about one salient fact I'd uncovered when looking for background information in preparation for interviews with the old lawman.

"Tell me, C.P., just who is Elfie Owens?"

The Bucket of Blood went completely silent, as if the saloon and everyone in it were hanging on his reply. "Elfie?" C.P. said in a dead voice. "Elfie is my only daughter," he said. "As you probably know, she was here in Seligman for a year. Fifteen years old at the time. I thought to give her a family, being as her ma'd died."

"Where is she now?"

"Only the Good Lord knows."

"You don't stay in contact?"

"Young man, I offered that girl my home to live in and me and Lizzie as her only kin. She wouldn't have it. She spent less than a year in high school here in Seligman before she run off with a railroad man."

I could tell he was wrought about the subject, but he continued. "She took off with a railroad man, I figure, though I have no proof. One day she's here, smiling at last where she'd been pouting ever since she come to Seligman. Only thing that'll change a woman that fast is a man. The next day she's gone, clothes packed in a big carpetbag, the one she'd brought her things in from St. Johns. Gone. I thought maybe she'd be in touch, but she's never contacted us. Never. I had a daughter, now I don't. That's all there is to it."

The year 1889 saw Commodore Owens step from behind his badge to become a horse rancher once more. His position as sheriff was taken over by the newly elected St. George Creaghe, who had once been Commodore's bondsman.

That same year, Red McNeil, whom Commodore had never captured, was taken into custody in Ogden, Utah, after robbing a saloon and shooting a patron in the leg. He was sent to Sugar House Prison in Utah to serve a ten-year sentence. While there, he studied, and after his release in 1899, he became a hydraulic engineer, never again riding the outlaw trail.

Commodore ran again for sheriff of Apache County in 1892 as an independent because he could not get the Democratic Party to back him as its candidate. Republican W. R. Campbell won, and immediately hired Commodore Perry Owens as his chief deputy. From the few records that exist, I assume he spent his time apprehending lawbreakers.

On August 8, 1893, scarcely a year after becoming chief deputy of Apache County, Commodore was appointed Deputy U.S. Marshal by William Kidder Meade, U.S. Marshal for Arizona Territory. His term was defined as to continue during Marshal Meade's continuance in office unless sooner revoked. Newspapers of the time carry several references to Commodore Owens as he acted in his capacity as a lawman. One man he arrested was Juan Garviso, who was found guilty of manslaughter in the saloon brawl and shooting death of Deputy Sheriff Edward Wright. Garviso got eight years in Yuma because he confessed.

Compare that to Charles C. Waggoner, who killed Issac Lee. He did not confess, and after a lengthy trial, he was sentenced to forty-five years in prison.

Will Barns, Commodore's friend and a witness to the Holbrook shootout, was elected to the Territorial Legislature in November 1894. He immediately went to work trying to get Apache County divided into Navajo to the west and Apache to the east. As a result, Navajo County came into being on March 21, 1895, carved from Apache County. Governor Louis C. Hughes then appointed C. P. Owens sheriff of the new county. He took his oath of office on April 1, 1895, and he kept his Deputy U.S. Marshal's badge.

Unlike during his term as Apache County sheriff, the newspapers referred to Commodore as "Navajo County's efficient sheriff."

Twenty years ago, newspapers quite often carried snippets of information that Sheriff C. P. Owens had captured someone, was taking some criminal to jail, or was returning from such a trip. One such, for example, noted that one F. H. Bloodgood was conducted to the territorial prison to serve two years, having been found guilty of "seduction."

Owens's undersheriff, by the way, was Robert Hufford, a nephew. As Owens had little formal education, he tended to surround himself with those who did. Hufford was once such, and he penned much of the official correspondence from the county sheriff's office.

W. K. Meade resigned his U.S. Marshal position July 1, 1897, which automatically terminated Commodore Owens's deputyship, and marked the end of his career as an officer of the law.

A day or two after Commodore Perry Owens died, the Phoenix Sun picked up an obituary article from the Associated Press. It trends to the hyperbole but it also is a mighty good tribute to the man.

Romantic Figure of Pioneer Days Has Passed From Stage of Action

Seligman, Ariz. June 25.— A romantic figure of Arizona's pioneer days has just passed in the person of Commodore Perry Owens, cattleman, sure-shot, dashing Indian fighter, and fearless sheriff, who died here.

With long waving hair, a pleasing personality and dignified carriage, Commodore Owens carved a spectacular career on Arizona's tables of history.

Owens was born in Indiana and came to Arizona via Texas and New Mexico in 1882, to become a range foreman of a cattle company at Navajo Springs.

In a single-handed battle with three Navajo Indians who were stealing the company's cattle, Owens killed the trio. Then followed numerous clashes with the red raiders, many of whom fell before his Henry rifle. In time the Indians came to believe he bore a charmed life and gave him a wide berth, since despite the frequent battles with them, he never received a wound.

In 1886 when outlaws throughout Apache County were defying the law, Owens was elected sheriff, and, backed by Judge Robert E. Morrison, now of Prescott, he obtained indictments against 16 of the most notorious thieves and murderers.

While the grand jury was reporting the true bills, a dozen or so outlaws fled the country rather than face the new sheriff. The latter tracked three of the remainder to the Blue River and there, when they were resisting arrest they were felled by the guns of Sheriff Owens and his posse. A fourth member of the gang, Phin Clanton, was trapped, captured, and sentenced to 10 years in prison.

Perhaps Owens's most spectacular battle was one fought at Holbrook, where the sheriff killed Andy Cooper, a notorious bad man, and two companions. Owens had been told that the trio had taken refuge in a house near the railroad tracks. He rode down the street to the building, walked to the door and rapped for admission, with his rifle held at his right hip. Cooper opened the door and attempted to draw a revolver but the sheriff fired from the hip. Cooper fell badly wounded. At the same moment another shot rang out from behind from the gun of one of Cooper's men, the bullet missing the sheriff's head. With his back to his second assailant, Owens threw his rifle over his shoulder and fired. The outlaw dropped mortally hurt.

As the sheriff retreated a few steps he saw a man through the window maneuvering for a shot and again the sheriff's rifle spoke. The outlaw inside fell to the floor and died within a few minutes. It was Cooper, who had been shot when he opened the door.

Then the third desperado made his appearance, running around the corner of the house with his revolver raised to fire, but before he could pull the trigger Owens shot and the last of the gang died in his tracks.

Owens served but one term as sheriff of Apache County, but it was said that at the end of this tenure of office every outlaw in the county had been driven out, killed or arrested.

For a short while the ex-sheriff served as an express messenger, but later he entered business on his own account and died peacefully in commercial harness.

As I said, the article varies from the true facts that I uncovered in my searching for the true story of C. P. Owens.

I have written the story of Commodore Perry Owens as it happened, taking as my sources newspapers of the day, of which there was a large collection in the morgue at the Phoenix Sun. For a while after the gunfight in Holbrook, editors of newspapers in Apache County seemed to take umbrage with Commodore Owens, wondering in print why the county needed law officers who walked around with abbreviated cannons on their hips. Still, I could not help but notice that although St. George Creaghe shunned C. P. Owens while serving as Apache County sheriff, the moment his successor, W. R. Campbell became sheriff, he hired C.P. as his chief deputy. Why would he do so if C.P. were not an efficient effective peace officer?

Barely one half year after C.P. became chief deputy sheriff of Apache County, he was appointed Deputy U.S. Marshal by William K. Meade, U.S. Marshal for Arizona. Again, of all the men in Arizona, why did Meade choose C. P. Owens?

I repeat this information to make a point. Commodore Perry Owens was seen by his fellow lawmen an honest, trustworthy man who was extraordinarily effective as an officer of the law.

I found him straightforward and honest in telling me his side of the life of Commodore Perry Owens. It pained me to see him lose his mental faculties, and I would have liked to have attended his funeral. However, I heard Elizabeth Owens decided to take C.P.'s body to Albuquerque for burial. Only later did I find out that he was actually buried in Flagstaff. It seems heavy rains in June of 1919 served to wash out several bridges between Seligman and Albuquerque, so Lizzie buried C.P. in Flagstaff, where the train had been shunted to a siding.

While C.P. died of natural causes, some of those who lived in the wild years of Apache County were not so lucky. Frank Wattron, justice of the peace and druggist, died of an overdose of laudanum. He took the tincture of opium to help himself sleep. J. D. Houck, who convinced C.P. to come to Arizona in the first place, took strychnine in May 1921, and died just two years after Commodore.

Lizzie Owens, who was twenty-two when she married fifty-year-old C. P. Owens in 1901, still lives in Seligman to this day.

Alexander Evanston
Phoenix Sun
December 1921

Author's Comment

Many have written about Commodore Perry Owens, most of whom I have read, some in unpublished manuscripts of their memories. Help came from the Wells Fargo Bank History Department, Arizona Historical Society, and authors such as Earle R. Forrest, Will C. Barnes (who witnessed the Holbrook fight), Dana Coolidge, Jo Jeffers, Harold Waite, George Crosby Jr., and David Grassé, who wrote the most comprehensive book concerning Commodore Perry Owens ever—*The True, Untold Story of Commodore Perry Owens*. Still, although based on history, I have written a novel. And, thanks to those who have gone before, it carries a glimmer of truth.

About the Author

Charles T. Whipple, an international prize-winning author, uses the pen name of Chuck Tyrell for his Western novels. Whipple was born and reared in Arizona's White Mountain country only 19 miles from Fort Apache. He won his first writing award while in high school, and has won several since, including a 4th place in the World Annual Report competition, a 2nd place in the JAXA Naoko Yamazaki Commemorative Haiku competition, the first-place Agave Award in the 2010 Oaxaca International Literature Competition, and the 2011 Global eBook Award in western fiction. Raised on a ranch, Whipple brings his own experience into play when writing about the hardy people of 19th century Arizona. Although he currently lives in Japan, Whipple maintains close ties with the West through family, relatives, former schoolmates, and readers of his western fiction. Whipple belongs to Western Fictioneers, Western Writers of America, Arizona Authors Association, American Society of Journalists and Authors, Asian American Journalists Association, and Tauranga Writers Inc.